BLUE FLAGS

BLUE FLAGS

Ralph Mason

LUMINARE PRESS
WWW.LUMINAREPRESS.COM

Blue Flags
Copyright © 2020 by Ralph Mason

This book is a work of fiction. References to real people, events, establishments, organizations, or locales are intended only to provide a sense of authenticity and are used fictitiously. All other characters, and all incidents and dialogue, are drawn from the author's imagination and are not to be construed as real.

Printed in the United States of America

Luminare Press
442 Charnelton St.
Eugene, OR 97401
www.luminarepress.com

LCCN: 2021911713
ISBN: 978-1-64388-553-7

To Bob, Sarah, Isabel and Janet

CHAPTER 1

The explosion was heard or felt everywhere. To me, a nineteen-year-old engineer cadet lying in my bunk on the main deck amidships, the thud seemed to have emanated from somewhere deep in the bowels of the vessel and was accompanied by a shuddering of the entire 10,000-ton motor ship. I realized immediately that something had gone seriously wrong but Chief Engineer James Robinson sitting in his cabin one deck above, knew immediately what had happened. He had experienced the same effects once before, over twenty years previously. He jumped up and dialed the Captain on the ships phone.

"What in god's name was that, Jim?" The Captain's voice was strained.

"Tony, I believe we just had a crankcase explosion. It's big trouble. I'm on my way to the engine room right now, whoever was down there is likely critically injured. Get the nurse and sick bay mobilized and close the watertight doors, we've got a fire to put out." The ship had lost all way and was wallowing in the heavy swell of the Indian Ocean. They were approximately 1,500 miles from the nearest port and from the assistance of a tugboat if that was going to be needed.

Word quickly spread around the ship of the serious injuries to two of the engineering crew members, a Pakistani oiler and the third engineer who had both been on watch at the time of the explosion. A junior engineer also on watch had been down the propeller shaft tunnel to pump the stern gland bilge. The blast wave from the explosion had largely dissipated by the time it reached him and he was able to escape by using the vertical ladder from the bilge valve area up to the poop. Although badly shaken up, he avoided injury. The oiler soon died from the head trauma and burn injuries he had received when he was struck by a door blown off the side of the crankcase by the explosion. The third engineer was also seriously burnt and concussed. When I was eventually allowed down into the engine room, the smell of burning oil was overpowering, I could not believe the havoc the explosion had caused. I was scared witless, there was still a fire burning even though the automatic fire suppression system inside the crankcase had been activated. The fire team, including the Chief Engineer, appeared to be getting the upper hand on the flames which they were fighting with foam filled fire extinguishers. The fire was eventually put out about two hours after the explosion. Fortunately, of the three diesel generators in the engine room, only one had been put out of action by the explosion and so we still had electric power all over the ship. But the vast main diesel engine used to drive the single propeller that could move the ship through the water at up to an 18-knot speed, was totally disabled. This 8,000-horsepower behemoth was over five stories high and filled the center of the engine room for a distance of 70 feet fore and aft. It soon became clear what had caused the explosion. A white metal bearing where side rods connected the upper piston of the opposed piston engine to the crankshaft, had failed. The metal-to-metal contact had generated sufficient heat to vaporize oil in the crankcase and ultimately a spark had ignited the flammable oil gas.

CHAPTER 2

My name is Philip Edward Marlin, I go by Phil. At the age of thirteen, I had left prep school and gone to the Nautical College at Pangbourne in Berkshire. I can't really remember why I went there. Perhaps it was because a friend of our family had a son who had gone there, and they had told my mother and father that it was a good place for a teenager to be schooled. Founded in 1917 by Sir Thomas Devitt, the basic objective of the school was to ready young men for a seagoing career as officers in the British merchant navy, although a small proportion of students each year were admitted to the Royal Naval College at Dartmouth. The all-boys boarding school was fairly heavy on discipline, naval working or dress uniform was always worn, and quite quickly turned me from an overweight pudgy schoolboy into a lean, reasonably well muscled, young man. At Port Jackson, the entry division of the school, we were woken with a bugle call at 6.50 am every morning except Sunday, before being herded out for a two-mile run in all weathers other than heavy snow. When we returned straggling in from the run, we were sprayed with cold water from a hose in a communal shower. One of the cadet leaders, who were generally seventeen years old, controlled the hose and at times seemed to be enjoying his job. We were entirely subject to the orders of the cadet officers that included, for each of four divisions at the school, a Chief Cadet Captain, Cadet Captains and Cadet Leaders. There was also a Chief Cadet Captain of the College, the top dog of all the cadet officers. They oversaw all our non-classroom and non-sport activities and chivvied us along at all times. After the cold spray, we had to make up our bunk style beds, get dressed in the uniform of the day, clean shoes, position lanyards, and generally get into presentable shape before assembling in a gun room. Many kids found the need to do these chores in a fixed short time, overwhelming. They would receive minor punishment until such time as they got everything done in the allotted time. We would then be ordered into the mess hall or dining room for breakfast which our young bodies devoured in less than twenty minutes. After a short break for bathroom functions, there were no doors on the toilets and one quickly adapted to a less modest defecation routine, we were marched up to the main school to start the academic day. The school curriculum included all the traditional subjects, Mathematics, Physics, English Language, English Literature, French, History, Geography, Divinity, but also included Seamanship and Navigation. Ordinary Level national examinations were taken at age fifteen and Advanced Level examinations at age seventeen. Afternoons were consumed with sports of all kinds but mostly focused on rugby and field hockey in the winter terms, and cricket, tennis, sailing and rowing in the summer. The river Thames was a few miles from the school's grounds, and a boathouse on the riverbank was the headquarters for the watersports.

After an initial year at Port Jackson, I was assigned to a more senior division called Macquarie. There were two other senior divisions, Hesperus and Harbinger, and there was a healthy rivalry between these divisions in intra mural sports. These division names were based upon the names of Devitt & Moore sailing ships that ventured to Australia in the 19th century. Every Sunday, the entire school assembled in dress uniform on the parade ground and marched around in front of the adult teachers and officers. The parade was led by the college drum, fife, and bugle band. Being a fairly big individual, I was by this time six feet one inches tall and 12 stone 12 pounds in weight, I wound up carrying the big bass drum and beating out the time for marching. I didn't always get it quite right and on occasion had the entire parade in a marching shambles. But eventually, I became a Cadet Captain and the drum major, the guy who led the parade holding a long golden staff. It was amazing because I have always had zero musical instrument talent.

Although intended primarily as an early training ground for deck officers responsible for a ship's movements in port and over the oceans, I knew that I was bound for the engine room and not the bridge. This was because of minor color blindness and my father's engineering background. This was somewhat frustrating to the school's executive officer, for at age seventeen, after a bad bout of health with peritonitis, I had entered the examination and won the open navigation prize and took home the new sextant that was awarded to the winner. Of course, I could and would never use a sextant or celestial navigation in the engineering side of the merchant navy, and I eventually sold the instrument to another graduating cadet. In later life I realized that being sent to a boarding school had probably been good for me. The discipline and structure of everyday life left little time for getting into trouble. Cardinal sins at the school were bad swearing (fuck was not a word to be used without serious repercussions), smoking (punishable ultimately by expulsion), homosexual relations (also punishable by expulsion but somewhat evident, perhaps more in the form of playing with each other, when sleeping in a dormitory holding thirty young men reaching sexual maturity), fighting, stealing, answering back or not responding to a cadet officer or member of the teaching staff. Other minor offenses were adjudicated by the cadet officers and could result in a thrashing across the rear with a stick. In true English public-school fashion, I had had little opportunity to mingle with the opposite sex, and this I'm sure, led to significant shyness and incompetence in my early dealings with females. This was probably the least attractive part of going to an all-boys boarding school.

Upon leaving the Nautical College, I had been hired by a venerable British company that owned thirty-six cargo vessels that operated as the Blue Flags Line. All the ships had a similar silhouette with a single prominent white funnel on each side of which were painted two blue triangular flags. The initiation to the company was a training program called a sandwich course, which involved two years of engineering studies, followed by eighteen months at sea and then twelve months in the company's workshops in Birkenhead. Following successful completion of the sandwich course, cadets would be promoted to the lowest rank of engineering officer and would be assigned to one of the company's vessels. The company's headquarters were in Liverpool, across the Mersey River from Birkenhead, and so they used a local technical college for the first part of the course which involved studying for an Ordinary National Diploma in Marine Engineering.

It wasn't until I was over eighteen and studying at the Riversdale Technical College in suburban Liverpool, that I had anything even approaching a relationship with the opposite sex. Her name was Joan McDonald, and she was enrolled at a nearby physical education teachers training college. Her dark hair and slightly pointed features were the initial attraction, but after going out with her a few times and getting a good night hug and kiss, I became aware of her lithe well-proportioned body and inviting breasts. And when we did kiss, I could feel her tremble and quiver. But being as incompetent as I was, I had no clue as to how to get her to give me access to her young body, which of course at that age, was a strong desire. I also grew quite fond of her and I thought, she of me. But that proved to be an error, as on my second voyage with the mail we received at Port Elizabeth, I received a 'Dear John' letter with some strange language about her mother telling her not to get involved with someone who would be away for months at a time. She never said it directly in the letter, but it was clear she had dumped me. I was quite upset, but with the emotional restraint that had been a feature of my British upbringing and schooling, I gave no sign of discomfort to my fellow cadets. And the first time we got some shore leave on the trip, I met a young nurse in Singapore. Five or six of us from the ship went to a swimming pool operated by the hospital where the nurses worked. They were all from the UK and clearly in desperate need of some male company. As we entered the pool area, many of the girls, for they were all noticeably young, looked at us and got up from their towels or deckchairs and came over to welcome us. We all looked at each other and smiled, then one of the girls broke the embarrassed silence and we all seemed to be talking at once. What ship were we off? How long were we going to be in port? How long had they been working at the hospital? Was there somewhere we could get a beer? We soon paired off though unfortunately, there were not enough of us for all the girls. I found myself with a somewhat plain faced girl who made up for it with a great looking figure and a very pleasant personality. She was easy to talk to and quickly dispelled my normal shyness. She was wearing a modest bikini, but it still showed her breasts off to great advantage.

"Where are you from?" she asked.

"I was born in Birmingham," I answered.

"Well, we were almost neighbours. I'm from Wolverhampton."

"I'm sorry, I never asked you your name," I blushed a little. I felt it should have been my first question, but I was having a hard time concentrating on our conversation. At age nineteen, the hormones were raging, and I was having difficulty taking my eyes off her bosom.

"Kelly, Kelly Jameson. My grandfather was Irish, but my family has lived north of the Black Country for many years. What's your name?"

"Phil Marlin, pleased to meet you, Kelly." She put out her hand and almost reflexively, I grasped hers. It was not a handshake, because she led me away to deckchairs on a corner of the concrete area around the pool where there was some shade.

"You look like you should stay out of the sun. Your skin is a very British white." She smiled as she spoke, and the plain face suddenly became attractive. "Can I get you a drink, we only have pop and water I'm afraid, the hospital won't let us have beer down here although later we may be able to get a bottle. One of my friends is going out with a local boy who smuggles a case in for us sometimes."

"Pop would be fine," I said and as she walked off, her tight bottom moved nicely under the bikini. We sat and talked for a while and then got in the pool to cool off. It must have been close to 90 degrees even in the shade. When we got out of the pool she went and got me a towel from a large hamper. "I've only been in Wolverhampton a few times, mostly passing through on my way to and from Liverpool. Although one time I remember going to a Wolves match with my dad."

"Are you a big football fan?" she asked.

"Not really, but it's fun to go to a game now and again." We were both lying on our towels on the hard concrete. "What do you do for fun out here in Singapore and how long will you be here anyway?" She looked straight at me as she answered.

"There is not a lot to do for young British nurses. The hospital keeps real close tabs on us. Strict curfew, no smoking or drinking, etc. We get around some of it of course. I'm out here for a year as part of a training course. We are not fully registered nurses yet. But you lads off the ships are a godsend for us." She moved close to me and kissed my cheek. I lost my virginity to that sweet girl from Wolverhampton. A little later, she led me away from the pool to her dormitory, removed her own and my swimsuit, and, after rolling a condom onto me, quickly grasped and guided me into her willing and needy body. Her breasts were truly beautiful, not too big and sloppy, not too small and close to the chest, but a perfect pert and supple size. Her nipples were hard under my lips. As we left the dormitory on our way back to the pool, I noticed two other couplings further down the dormitory. Those poor nurses were really sex starved. After we left Singapore, I never saw the West Midlands girl again.

The motor vessel Olympus was the ship I was assigned to for my third voyage, which like the first two voyages, involved shipment of manufactured goods from Europe to the Far East, China and Japan, and a return loaded with natural resources such as rubber, copra, palm oil, tea, cocoa nut, and hides. I had boarded the Olympus at Birkenhead and our first port of call had been Dublin where we loaded thousands of cases of Guinness beer, which supposedly people in Asia believe is good for making babies. Then on to Rotterdam where we picked up more general cargo and a few passengers. In general, the vessels could accommodate between eight and twelve passengers in single and double cabins on the officer's deck level. As cadets, we only met the passengers in the officers dining room where breakfast, lunch and dinner were served by Chinese, Pakistani or Filipino waiters.

There were four cadets on the MV Olympus, two training to be deck officers, they were called midshipmen, and two for engineering. We all lived in a communal cabin with four bunk beds and an adjacent living area with fixed table and bench seats and vertical locker and cupboard space. A bathroom with shower, urinal and WC was also connected to the space. Considering we were the lowest of the low in officer terms and we were all in our nineteens and twenties, we were quite happy. The space was on the main deck well above the waterline, and three portholes provided plenty of light during the day. We were required to get into dress uniform for our meals and that could range from smart shorts and white shirt in the tropics, to dark navy blue suit with tie and white shirt, which is how we were dressed when the four of us trooped into dinner on the evening we sailed from Rotterdam. We normally sat with the third mate and the third engineer and were careful to keep our voices down. The Captain, Mr. Anthony Mosgrave, had, through the third mate, warned us to be on our best behavior while dining, and that included being seen but not heard. We were waiting to be served as the passengers had not yet entered the dining room. When they did, there was a collective but muted gasp from all at our table. The second passenger to enter the room was a strikingly beautiful woman perhaps thirty-five years of age, tall, blond hair swept back, and skin that almost glowed. Even in the suit she wore, it appeared she had only just boarded, her slim figure manifested a distinct bust line and hip and rear torso definition. She wore a string of small pearls around her neck, a single large diamond ring on her right hand, and a Hermes scarf loosely on her shoulders.

"Wow, that is one good looking piece of arse," John Grange, the other engineering cadet, whispered in my ear. "I wonder who she's with?"

"She's more than that," I whispered back. "She looks like a very expensive sexual companion for some lucky guy."

"Phil, I'm surprised at you," John raised his eyebrows as he spoke.

"Keep it down, Grange, you too Marlin." The third engineer stared directly at us both. A middle aged executive looking man, closely styled haircut, fine wool suit, flashy cufflinks, entered the dining room and walked to the lady's side. They moved to the Captain's table and sat.

"I guess she has a partner," I said. But as I looked at them, they barely glanced at each other and appeared to be more interested in other passengers at the table. Soon the remaining passengers entered the room followed by the Captain and the Chief Engineer. It looked like our passenger cabins would be full at least until our first stop at Durban in South Africa.

After leaving Rotterdam, we traversed the English Channel and then headed into the Bay of Biscay, a notoriously rough patch of ocean which even this mid-May, lived fully up to its reputation. After some sea sickness on my first voyage, I had become somewhat inured to the ship's motion provided I had a stomach full of bread or other carbohydrate. However, many of our twelve passengers, including the beautiful woman, went missing from the dining room and didn't return until we were off the coast of northern Spain, where the rough sea had abated.

CHAPTER 3

Colin McDonald was born in 1928 in the tiny village of Arisaig in the west highlands of Scotland. On the road and railway from Fort William to Mallaig and from there, the ferry to the Isle of Skye, Arisaig saw people passing through but rarely stopping. Colin's, father and mother, Douglas and Morag, were also born in the Arisaig area. Douglas had gone to sea at the age of 18 and had married Mary when he was 25. Colin was born one year later and was joined by two sisters within another three years. Arisaig offered much of the scenic beauty of the Scottish Highlands, quiet lochs, sparse pine forests, small woods of larch, oak, wild cherry, silver birch, hazel, beach and ash, a rocky shoreline with small sand coves and views of the isles of Rum, Eigg and Muck to the west, open hills rising to crags inland, and a quiet solitude for those seeking peace. But as a young man, after completing grammar school, Colin decided that the area was too quiet, insufferably so, and he needed to see the world beyond the borders of Scotland. At age 19, he was handsome in a modest way, he did not have film star looks, but his dark red hair, high forehead, and straight firm chin line, together with a lean eleven stone on a five-feet-ten-inch frame, made him an attractive young man. He had by nature, a positive outlook on life, but once an opinion formed in his mind, it was, just as in his father's case, hard to change or displace it.

 He knew that his father had worked for the Blue Flags shipping line based out of Liverpool and had ultimately become a Captain and had made many trips to the Far East. During the second world war, Douglas had survived the torpedoing of his Blue Flags vessel by a Japanese submarine in the South China Sea. Colin eventually persuaded his Dad to contact the shipping company and suggest that he Colin, would make an excellent addition to the company's ocean-going crew. Douglas had retired from Blue Flags, but his letter to Captain Thurmond at the company, was answered affirmatively by return. There was a position as a deck officer trainee waiting for Colin if he was able to make his way to Liverpool. It was clear that his dad was held in high esteem by the company, and this made Colin nervous. If he joined Blue Flags, would he be able to live up to his father's reputation? With train fare from his father, and a bag of food from his mother, he set out on what became a two-day trip to Liverpool. In took a whole day for him to reach Glasgow as he had to change trains at Fort William and the Glasgow train was very late. Thus, after walking from Glasgow Queen Street Station to Central Station, he had missed the last train to Liverpool, and he spent the night on a bench in a waiting room. In the morning he had just enough money for a cup of tea at the station before boarding the early train. He reached the Liverpool city address he had been given by his father, at 2.30 pm, and was immediately absorbed into the merchant navy world.

Colin took to the ocean-going life and soon became a junior deck officer standing watch with the second mate on one of the company's oldest ships powered by a reciprocating steam engine. His quarters were small and spartan, but this was of no import, he was intoxicated by the vastness of the open sea, by the exotic ports of the Orient, by the power of ocean storms, and by incredible black nights filled with an endless array of stars. He found no difficulty responding to the requirements of his seniors, even though he found some directives silly and petty. His studies on board included navigation including use of LORAN, seamanship, radar, and the specific characteristics of the Thalassa, a vessel that had survived the war but was nearing the end of her days. His computational capabilities were supplemented with practical observations of the sun and stars, and the use of electronic navigation methods. His navigation skills were soon on a par with other officers.

By age 25 he was a third mate on a much newer vessel in the company's fleet. After a four-month voyage, he returned to Arisaig for a month's leave and married Mary Dundas, a young woman from Edinburgh who was teaching at the local elementary school. He had met Mary several years before and had thought of her then as simply a young schoolteacher. But on a previous leave, he had somehow found himself talking to her at a Saturday night dance, and as they continued to talk, he began to realize that Mary had a fierce intelligence. It was only then that he began to look at her seriously and was stunned by her natural beauty. Why hadn't he seen this before? She had porcelain like smooth white skin and her eyes were unusually brown. When she looked straight at him, as she was wont to do when immersed in a serious conversation, he felt himself being drawn into their depths. He met her again for a walk the next afternoon. As she greeted him at their planned meeting point, he noted the outline of her figure. She was not thin, but neither was she in any way, plump. She had a noticeable bosom, a defined waistline and hips that seemed to flare out and complement her rear. They sat on some shoreside rocks, the wind was cold for early May, they both had woolen scarfs protecting their throats and necks. She wanted to know all about his time at sea. What was it really like being out on the ocean thousands of miles from land? Were all seaman rum swilling braggards who chased whores when in a port? He blushed at her question but could see that she was expecting an answer.

"Mary, where did you get that idea from?" he asked with a slight smile.

"Well, I have been in Leith a few times and I've seen men who certainly seemed to fit that description," she replied.

"Of course, there are some like that, but far from all. I have worked with many officers over the last few years, and I can think of only two or three that might fall into that category. Now deckhands may be a different story, what they do when they get some money in their hands and go ashore, is probably not fit for a lady's ears," Colin said.

"Colin, I'm not a prude, and I understand that men who are cooped up in a ship for weeks at a time with no female company, could try to seek such when they go ashore. But I would have thought that the dangers of getting some horrible disease, or being robbed or beaten or worse, would have discouraged them." Colin looked at her carefully as he considered his next words. She was young, how much did she know or understand of men's sexual needs? Was she a woman of the world, perhaps no longer a virgin? She certainly had not been sheepish in raising the subject.

"From my experience, the male sexual drive can become overpowering. Many men will take severe risks in attempting to satisfy that drive," he said.

"Are you one of those?" she asked. Her question dumfounded him. Now his normally pale cheeks had splotches of red. He looked away from her in embarrassment. "Colin, I'm sorry, that was a very personal question." She took his hand in hers. "You don't need to answer me. But of course, if you don't, my mind will start to imagine all kinds of things." Her last words had a cheeky tone and he looked at her and couldn't help laughing.

"Mary, sometimes you know, you are quite naughty." She still held his hand, and he could feel his heart pounding. She really was someone special. Quite suddenly she leaned towards him and lightly kissed his lips. Her kiss sent a shock through his entire body and particularly to his pelvic region. He put his arm around her and pulled her close. Their next kiss was the real thing, her mouth was sweet and tender, and he could feel her squirming a little as he gently pushed the tip of his tongue between her lips. Then her tongue was in his mouth and they were locked in a deep exchange.

"Wow," she exclaimed as she pulled away from him. "You seem to be in the needy class."

"I am, but I sense I'm not alone." She smiled at his words but didn't blush.

"You never answered my question," she looked quizzically at him.

"Perhaps another day Mary. What just happened kind of overwhelmed me." He also knew he could not get up yet. His erection was still strong and if he rose, he knew it would be noticeable. She got up and looked out to sea.

"I see some fishing boats out there. Making me feel ready for a good fish dinner. We could go dutch at the café. What do you think?" she said.

"Yes, let's go for an early dinner, but it will be my treat," he replied.

He didn't see her again until the next weekend which was his last before he would be off to sea again for at least four months. The weather had turned foul with rain squalls every few minutes and a cold biting wind from the north. This was a little unusual for late May but in this part of Scotland, stormy weather could and did occur at any time of the year. They tried walking out after she had finished at school. But the wind played havoc with their umbrellas and they soon retreated to her rented room in town.

"Is it OK for you to have visitors?" Colin asked.

"I don't know, I've never had a male one here before," she replied. She was busy lighting a fire and readying a kettle to place on the fireplace hob. The room contained two easy chairs, a tiny table with three wooden stools, a small bookcase with a few old dusty volumes, a twin bed, and a small sink with hot and cold water. There were two dark landscape paintings on the wall and heavy floor length curtains that were drawn back by the single window.

"There's a bathroom down the hall if you need it," she said. "The room is pretty plain isn't it, but it's all I can afford now. Once the fire gets going, it will warm up, but I have to crack open the window because of the fire and that creates a bit of a draft unless I draw the curtains." They sat staring into the fireplace as the flames grew around the kindling and the coal above started to catch on fire.

"How long will you be gone the next time you leave?" she asked.

"I have to go to Birkenhead to pick up my next ship on Tuesday. Not sure where we are headed yet, but it will probably be Hong Kong, Japan, Indonesia, and ports in those parts. Likely be four months."

"Do you miss home when you're away for so long?"

"A little, particularly my family, I'm very fond of my sisters. But," he hesitated, "I feel now that I'm going to miss you too." She got up from her chair and kneeled beside him and rested her head on his lap. He stroked her dark thick hair and leaned over to kiss the top of her head. Then he slid to the floor beside her and kissed her full on the mouth. The kiss lasted and she put her arms around his waist and pulled him close. His head fell to her sweater covered breast and instinctively he nuzzled into the warm softness. He felt her quiver, and he could feel the fast beating of her heart. She pulled his head up.

"Colin, there is something I must tell you," she whispered the words. He looked into her deep brown eyes and saw a trace of anguish. "I have been with a man before. I am not a virgin." There was silence in the room except for the crackling of the fire.

"Dear Mary, to respond to the question you asked me last week, I have been with other women. But they were not harlots and I'm sorry to say that one was married." Mary got up and went to a cupboard by the side of the bed. She put tea from a caddy into a small tea pot and then brought the pot with two cups over to the fireplace.

"I'm sorry, did I upset you? I thought it better to be truthful," he said. She busied herself making the tea and pouring two cups.

"Did you enjoy your dalliances?" Her words were not spoken in a judgmental manner.

"Errr, one yes, the other no," he answered. "Do you really want details?" He regretted the words as soon as he had uttered them. "Sorry, I guess I'm sensitive about such intimacies."

"I met a boy while I was at teacher's training college. It's funny, I have little feeling for him now and even at the time, I was not in love with him. But it was a warm summer's day on a deserted beach. We were sitting on a towel in the dunes at the back of the beach. We had been drinking earlier in the day, and I suppose I was half drunk. Anyway, the next thing I knew we were naked, and he was thrusting into me. I was so worried I would get pregnant. That would have been a disaster. But fortunately, I didn't." They drank their tea in silence. Then Mary got up, took his hand, and led him over to the bed. They sat side by side for a moment and then she stripped off her sweater, kicked off her shoes and socks and pulled down her skirt. Then she went around to the other side of the narrow bed and slid herself under the sheets and comforter. Colin quickly undressed. She had aroused him in a way that he had never experienced. He knew he should be tender and gentle, but there was a fierce need in his loins. The bed was very small for the two of them, but they soon became almost as one in a close embrace. He undid the clasp at the back of her brassiere and felt the wonderful pressure of her breasts against his chest. Then his hands were lowering her underwear. She helped, and then kicked the cotton out of the bed. God, she felt so good. He kissed her bosom as her hand went to his full erection. She stroked him.

"Colin, please pull out when you are close. I will finish you with my hand." Her words further inflamed him, and he moved on top of her. She was slick and he slid easily into her sheath. She moaned softly as he entered her and started thrusting. Within less than a minute he had to pull out and spurted his seed into her hands. The release was ecstatic. She slid out of his embrace, took a handkerchief from the nightstand, and walked naked to the wardrobe. He continued to marvel at her beauty. She donned a robe and disappeared out the door. He heard water running and then a toilet flush, a minute or so later and then she was naked back in bed with him and wiping him with the now clean but damp handkerchief.

"Was that good for you my dear, no, my darling?" she said.

"Am I really your darling? And it was deeply satisfying," his reply was fractured by his rapid breathing as he continued to recover from the intense orgasm. "But I don't think I have satisfied you yet." He remembered the time with the married woman. She was the wife of the French consul in some port in Indonesia, he couldn't recollect the name. She was thirty years older than him in age, but light years more experienced in the ways of love and sex. Her husband was in his seventies, fat and probably impotent. She had pulled Colin's hand between her legs and rotated it slowly and then more quickly and then she had arched her shaking body and let out an almost primal scream. Although he was ignorant of the specific details of a woman's anatomy, he knew from that coupling, that there was a seat of pleasure somewhere above the vagina. He moved his hand on to Mary's stomach and then gently lower until he encountered her pubic hair. She gradually spread her legs as he stroked the incredibly soft flesh on the inside of her thighs. Then he felt the slickness and brought it up from her vaginal entrance. She started to moan and squirm as he moved his hand around the area. He thought that he felt a little nub under his fingers, but he wasn't sure, and in any event, whatever he was doing, appeared to be having a thrilling effect on Mary.

"Oh, don't stop, don't stop," she moaned and then went almost rigid. It frightened him a little, was she alright? She was breathing rapidly, and she seemed to be flexing her hips, but then gradually she relaxed and clung to him. Then she was kissing his face and chest and stomach and phallus, which was quite rapidly gaining in size and rigidity.

"My, my, this fellow of yours certainly knows what he likes," she said. Colin burst out laughing.

"Well, it seems to me that a part of your anatomy has the same inclination," she punched his arm playfully in response.

As he walked back to his parent's house in the pouring rain, Colin knew that he had fallen in love with Mary. It wasn't just the sex, although that had been wonderful, but it was the sharp wit and intelligence, the incredible depth of her brown eyes, and the feeling that she really liked him, even loved him. What more could a man want in a wife he thought. Before he left, he wrote her a short letter for he knew that any letters he wrote to her from the ship would probably not reach her till he was back home again.

My Dearest Mary

> *I will truly miss you. I can't imagine anything more wonderful than being in your arms. I know I am asking a lot, but please wait for me to return in the Autumn. I will have an important question for you then.*
>
> *All my Love Colin*

On his walking way to the railway station on Tuesday morning, he pushed the letter under the front door of the house where she rented the room. His heart was heavy as he boarded the train for Glasgow, he wouldn't be seeing her again for such a long while. Would she wait for him? Did she feel about him the way he felt about her? But then the memory of their times together flooded his mind and he felt better. He knew that when he returned, he would ask her to marry him. And if she said yes, oh god she must say yes, he would want to get married right away, and he hoped she would feel the same.

CHAPTER 4

She did wait for him. When he asked the important question, she burst into tears and flung herself into his arms. Yes, and yes, they should marry right away. Her family came from Edinburgh for the nuptials and celebrations and Douglas, Morag and his sisters, and other family members in the area, made the quickly arranged ceremonies special. He borrowed his father's car for the five-day honeymoon, staying at a little hotel at Portree on the Isle of Skye. When he left for his next trip, and Mary went back to teaching at the school, they didn't know it, but she was pregnant. On the return voyage home, he had received a letter from her telling of her condition and when he returned, she was showing, and he could not believe that he would soon be a father. The pregnancy was going well although she had had some morning sickness in the early months. She had moved to the McDonald family house and was occupying Colin's room.

Colin quickly sensed that everything was not perfect in Mary's world. She was not a whiner, but within a few days of his return she expressed concern to him about her living arrangements. His family could not have been nicer to her, but she wanted a place of their own. Because Colin spent most of his life away from Arisaig, he had never really focused on the details of his home life. Now with Mary's concern and the baby on the way, he knew they needed to take some action. So, Mary and he rented a small cottage in town. It had running water and was connected to the town's sewers. He spent days re-plastering and repainting the two-bedroom one bath house, and within a week they had purchased some basic furniture which was soon delivered from Fort William, and they moved in.

Mary's next worry would be that Colin would be away when the baby was born. She was also starting to fret about having to give up her teaching job and how she would manage with the baby after the birth. Morag came to the rescue on all accounts. The grandma to be, assured Mary that they would take care of her and the baby if Colin were away, and that she would help with the new baby until Mary felt comfortable. She also told Mary that as a member of the local school board she would see to it that Mary could return to teaching as soon as she felt that she could. What she couldn't do was promise that Mary would go back to the Arisaig elementary school, she might have to take a position somewhere else in the area, possibly Mallaig. After eight hours labor, a healthy squalling Joan McDonald was born at the hospital in Fort William. At that precise time, Colin was in Sapporo Japan, over 5,000 miles away as the crow flies. He received a telegram when the ship docked in Osaka three days later. He was the father of a healthy 7 lb. 8 oz. baby girl. They had decided on the name Joan before he had left. If it had been a boy, it would have been John. And two years later John was born after a short and relatively easy labor.

At the age of 33, Colin became the youngest first mate in the Blue Flags company. He had passed all his written tests with flying colors and earned his 'tickets' in record time. It was on his first trip as the deputy to the Captain, that the accident occurred. He was supervising the loading of cargo at a remote port in British North Borneo when a rope sling parted, and a heavy pallet swung and hit him in the right hip. It was fortunate that the pallet had not hit his head, for if it had, he would have had a badly cracked skull as a minimum. But as it was, his hip had been crushed and he had lost some blood. Because of the ship's remote location, it was not feasible to radio for an air ambulance, there was no airfield within fifty miles of the port site. He was taken to the ship's sick bay and given morphine by the orderly. The pain had been greater than anything he had ever experienced. After conferring with the fleet operations department by radio link, the Captain rerouted the ship and immediately set sail for Singapore. They would come back later for the remainder of the cargo they had been loading. It took a day and a half to reach the port and Colin had been kept sedated the whole time. There was little else that could be done for him on the ship other than cleaning and dressing the nasty flesh scrape and wound. They had no facilities to x-ray or operate on his shattered pelvic bones. An ambulance crew was waiting on the dock, and they quickly removed him, started a blood transfusion, and took him to Singapore General Hospital. He remained in the hospital for over eight weeks during which he had three separate operations on his right hip. The doctors had cautioned him that he might never walk again without a crutch, but as his physical therapy progressed, he became determined to walk without support. He started to crab walk, dragging his right foot behind him. Eventually he was able to lift the foot and take short steps forward. At this point he was discharged from the hospital and put on board a company vessel headed to the UK. He was a given a single cabin normally occupied by a passenger and spent hours and hours on deck slowly walking and building strength back into his right hip.

The company had notified Mary as soon as the news of the accident had reached Liverpool. She wanted desperately to be with her husband but the trip to Singapore would take many weeks and she had two small children to take care of. The company had offered to take her at no charge, on the next company vessel headed for Singapore. But when she was finally able to speak to Colin on a phone line that sounded as if he were at the bottom of the ocean, he told her it was much more important that she stay home with the children, that he was progressing and would be home soon, and that she should not worry about him. Of course, he was not home soon, and she did constantly worry about him. She tried to call him in the hospital at least once a week, but often the calls never went through properly or the lines were so bad that they could barely understand each other.

Colin began to think about his future. Could he remain a deck officer with his infirmity or perhaps worse yet, his disability? As the vessel headed north towards the western tip of Africa, he realized that his days as a seagoing officer with the Blue Flags Line might well be over. The company had been incredibly good to him so far, but he wondered just how far they would go. Would there be a shore job that he could undertake, and would he want that anyway? He also began thinking about the accident. Why had the sling lifting the pallet, failed? He knew that all the equipment for hoisting that was kept on the ship was inspected regularly, and any signs of chafing or damage to a rope sling would immediately be reason to discard and scrap it. No, for some reason, the load was being lifted with a sling from the lighter that was alongside having its cargo being loaded directly onto the Blue Flags vessel. That was against company policy but somehow it had happened.

CHAPTER 5

Fiona Marchbanks had met Jacob Bakker on the terrace of a hotel in St. Moritz. She had been a model in her twenties and remained, in her mid-thirties, a strikingly beautiful woman. She was a natural blond, she had never used hair dye of any kind, and her skin had a glowing sheen particularly when she had a light tan. She had skied most of the morning but had decided to have lunch and then perhaps relax with a book in the afternoon. She had come to St. Moritz alone, having just received the divorce decree from her second husband. She had done fairly well in the settlement, at least well enough that she had a home in England and money enough to take a nice vacation in Switzerland. She noticed the man eating alone across the terrace and their eyes met for a second before both returned their gazes to the fabulous view of the Alps that lay before them. As she continued eating the fresh salad topped with goat cheese, she sensed a shadow cross the table and she looked up to see the somewhat handsome well-groomed man smiling down at her.

"Madam, excuse me for interrupting your lunch, but I couldn't help admiring the bracelet on your left wrist. It appears to be an exceptionally fine piece of antique jewelry." His English was good, but he had a strong accent.

"Errr yes, it has been in my family for many years," she said as she looked up into his incredibly blue eyes.

"I am in the fine gem business. Would it be possible for me to look at the piece more closely? It appears to be of the vary highest quality." She was stunned by the personal request, but his eyes had a pleading quality. She hesitated a moment. "I would be pleased to give you an informal appraisal of the value if you would be interested," he said. She nodded to him. Although the piece had come from her mother, she didn't really like it and thought that if it was of sufficient value, she might try to sell it.

"OK, but you won't run off with it will you?" She half smiled as she spoke the words.

"No, no please. I have no ill intent, just a real interest in the jewelry, and the wearer." Wow, this guy was a smooth operator, she thought. But he was rather charming. She motioned to him to sit at her table as she removed the bracelet from her wrist and handed it to him. He took it gently and rotated it in his hands. Then he reached to the inside pocket of his cashmere blazer and withdrew a magnifying glass. She watched him, fascinated by the way he examined each stone, the gold links, and the settings.

"Well, what do you make of it?" she said.

"It is, as I thought, a piece of exceptional quality made, I would estimate, in the late 19th century, perhaps around 1890. The diamonds are old cut, they were cut by hand and have 58 facets including the culet at the base of each. They all appear to be at least VVS1 or flawless with D or E color. Beautiful stones in platinum settings. I would estimate the total carat weight at something close to five. But it's the overall design of the piece that caught my eye, quite extraordinary, and very rare." He handed the piece back to her.

"And?" she asked.

"Well, the value is hard to estimate because of the rarity of the design. Based upon the gems and the gold in the links of the bracelet, it would sell for about US$6,000, but I would place its true value closer to US$10,000. It is, to someone in the business, a stunning example of late 19th century jewelry. Of course, beauty is in the eye of the beholder. Would you be interested in selling it?" He looked at her quizzically.

"I might. Although it is a family piece, I personally have never liked it that much. The diamonds don't seem to have the sparkle that I would expect," she said.

"That is because of the way they were cut. Not so much sparkle but perhaps more warmth?" he replied. "And talking of warmth, it is getting a little cool out here, could I buy you a warming drink inside at the bar?"

She wasn't quite sure how it happened, but two hours later they were naked in her bed having just made love. It must be a reaction to the finality of the divorce, she thought. But his lovemaking had been tender, and she knew she wanted to spend more time with him, whoever he was. His name was Jacob Bakker and she soon learned that he too was recently divorced, from a German woman who he had been married to for seven years. He lived in Antwerp and was the part owner of a firm that traded fine quality gems, mostly diamonds. He appeared to be quite wealthy and over the next few days he hosted her to numerous fine meals and trips, never allowing her to spend a franc. As the end of her vacation approached, she needed to get back to London to wrap up some issues related to the settlement, she invited him to visit her at the flat she owned in Kensington. He readily agreed, and so a relationship began. They neither of them had children and so they spent their time together talking, eating, visiting the theatre, making love, and generally quite enjoying each other's company. She realized early on that she was not in love with Jacob. He was a friendly sexual companion, and she found his company generally tolerable and even, at times, fun and exciting. But he had a few, to her, strange hang ups. He would not eat red meat, he would not fly, he was deathly afraid of aircraft, and he hated to use condoms. He had used one on that first afternoon in St. Moritz, but she quickly found out that he would much rather not, and he appeared relieved when she told him he should not be concerned because she was taking birth control pills.

During her first visit to his home in Antwerp, he had asked whether she would like to accompany him on an upcoming voyage to Singapore. He didn't indicate why he was going to Singapore, but she figured it had something to do with his business. Four weeks later she met him in Rotterdam and boarded what to her looked like a grimy cargo vessel. But the cabin was comfortable and the food on the boat was quite good. Once they were south of Gibraltar and headed down the west coast of Africa, the Suez Canal was still closed after the six-day war, she was able to start sunbathing and relaxing on the deck, and the cruise became pleasant. They ate at the Captain's table and spirits and wine were very reasonably priced. Not that she paid a penny, Jacob paid her fare and covered all expenses. She noticed that every time he left and returned to the cabin, he unlocked a small suitcase and looked inside it.

"Jacob, what on earth is in that suitcase that you are checking so carefully?" Her inquisitiveness had finally overcome her.

"My dear, it's the reason for the trip. I am couriering a shipment of gem grade diamonds to my agent in Singapore. There are in a velvet bag in the suitcase. You know I will not fly, so hence the reason for the cruise. I actually quite enjoy the leisurely trip, and with you it has become a real pleasure."

"So are the contents of the bag very valuable?" she asked.

"Close to US$5 million," he said. Fiona gasped.

"My god Jacob, shouldn't you have some additional security traveling with you?"

"I have thought about that, but the less attention I draw to myself the better."

"But shouldn't you put the bag in the ship's safe, wouldn't it be more secure there?"

"Again, in requesting that it be put in the safe, I would be drawing attention to it and me. No, I think it's best this way and in fact I've been doing this for years."

"How many times have you made this trip?" Fiona asked.

"Too many to count, although I've only been on Blue Flags twice before. I used another shipping line for several years, but their service deteriorated, so I switched."

"Couldn't you just send the diamonds in a package with special handling?" She looked hard at Jacob as she made the suggestion, but she saw immediately that it was a silly idea. "No, I suppose you would not want to let the bag out of your possession. But what about when the steward comes in here to clean the cabin, he could easily find the bag?"

"That's why I lock the bag in my suitcase and keep the case in the closet. I would know immediately if that case had been moved or tampered with. And I check to make sure the bag is in there every time we leave and return to the cabin, you know that. The bag has a special seal on it, and if anyone had tried to open it, I would know immediately. And we are on a ship, if the bag had been opened or went missing, where would the thief hide whatever was taken? We could have the ship searched from stem to stern."

"Well, it makes me a little nervous to know that we are traveling with such a valuable cargo."

"Fiona, the only other people in the world who know about this is my partner in Antwerp. Even the agent in Singapore doesn't know exactly when I will arrive or how I will get there. So please don't worry yourself, let's just enjoy the trip."

Fiona found the return trip from Singapore tiring and tiresome. She enjoyed Jacob's company, but the return voyage would take over four weeks and there was something about being together in such a confined space for such a long time that got on her nerves. They only had one port of call for cargo on the way home and that was at Trincomalee in Ceylon. The vessel was loading a shipment of tea at the port and she and Jacob only had one day to do some sightseeing and sunbathing on a beautiful palm tree lined beach. She needed the break badly and the beach was noticeably quiet, so she took off her one-piece swimsuit and lay on the large towel they had brought from the ship.

"You look gorgeous my dear, but shouldn't you put sun cream on to prevent getting burnt particularly in those places that don't normally see the sun?" Jacob's enquiry stimulated a tingling between her legs, and she nodded.

"Please, rub firmly on my legs, back, rear, breasts and stomach, but please go gently down below." He did as he was told. He had found that it was always better to do as Fiona wished, any attempt to dissuade her or change her opinion on almost any matter, was fruitless. As he reached her breasts, she started to raise her rear off the towel, and when he delicately applied cream to her mons and labia, she started to moan. He had found that she was a natural blonde, and she kept her pubic hair short and neatly trimmed. She had told him that she used to get a Brazilian wax, but she gave up on it because of the pain involved in the procedure. And her man of that moment had said that she felt and looked like a child and that he preferred her with hair.

"Do you see anyone on the beach?" Fiona asked. Jacob looked around.

"There is another couple a long way down the beach to our left. I think they may be doing what I think you are about to suggest."

"Get your swimsuit off, I need your cock inside me." He needed no further invitation, and quickly obliged her.

CHAPTER 6

As the ship approached Liverpool, Colin McDonald's concern about his future with Blue Flags had grown to an obsession. What would he do if he had to leave the company? How would he support Mary and the children? His whole working life had been aimed at becoming a Captain in the merchant navy, he had no other skills. He would have to start over in some new profession. Mary would have to continue teaching. The thought of that future dogged his outlook, caused depression and many sleepless nights, and made him feel almost physically sick. He could now walk but only slowly and with a pronounced limp to the right. He knew that his condition would not be acceptable to the company. Their deck officers needed to be fit, upstanding and capable of taking on arduous duty if necessary. He knew that however hard he tried to make his case, they would never let him go to sea as an officer again.

It was a grey overcast morning as the vessel approached the dock. Liverpool was not the most attractive port environment, but his heart was lifted by the sight of Mary, the two children, and his mother and father standing on the dock and looking anxiously up. He started waving madly and they soon picked him out and started waving back. He was suddenly overcome with emotion, tears welled from his eyes and dripped onto the ships railing, he had forgotten how much he had missed them all. As soon as the ship berthed and the gangplank had been lowered to the dock, the McDonalds climbed up to the boat deck and embraced Colin. There were many tears amongst the hugs and kisses, and he immediately felt his depression lifting. They all crowded into his small cabin, his son and daughter sitting on his lap and the adults sitting on the one other chair and the bed. It was wonderful to have his family around him, but he really wanted some private and intimate time with Mary. He needed to tell her all that had happened to him, all his worries about the future, how much he had missed her conversation, and how much he had missed her warm and loving body.

"You have been gone such a long time, and we were all so concerned about you," Morag said. "How did they treat you in the hospital?"

"It seemed as if I was there for an age, but it was actually just eight weeks. The doctors and surgeons who worked on me, I have plates and screws in my right hip, were excellent. I'm sure the nurses got fed up with me. I must have showed them the picture of Joan and John twenty times. But I got to see snaps of their families and came to know one or two of them quite well," Colin answered.

"Not too well I hope," Mary stared at him as she spoke but then broke into a big smile.

"I have been speaking to Captain Thurmond," Douglas said. "He wants to see you at 9 am in the morning." Colin looked inquiringly at his father. "I'll tell you more about our conversation later," Douglas continued. "But why don't we get you off the ship and into our hotel where we all can get a drink and some lunch. We plan to take the kiddies to the zoo this afternoon, give you and Mary some time together." Colin nodded gratefully at his dad. He knew what a man who had been away from his wife for months, wanted. The lunch tasted wonderful, and the two children both behaved admirably. Soon after lunch, his parents and the children left, and he and Mary were finally alone. As they slowly walked hand in hand back to the hotel room, Colin felt stirrings that he had not experienced for over three months. Being severely injured, the hospital time with the three operations, and then the physiotherapy, had not been conducive to that feeling of well-being associated with sexual thoughts and desires.

"You seem to be walking quite well," Mary said.

"I am getting a little stronger every day, but I do get tired easily," Colin replied. "How are things going at home? How are you managing with teaching and the two children? I thought about you all so much after the accident. I really made me realize what is important in life."

"I was so worried about you. You know the company offered to send me on the next ship to Singapore at no charge. I sorely wanted to be with you, but I wasn't sure that Douglas and Morag could look after Joan and John for an extended time. They can be a handful. And I must admit that I didn't want to abandon the teaching job again. I was lucky to get it back after having two babies, but Morag has much influence with the school board." Colin hugged her close as they entered the room. He looked over at the bed and she squeezed his arm.

"I think I need it just as much as you do," Mary said. "Get undressed, I want to look at your hip first." Colin sat in a chair, took off his jacket and then removed his trousers, shoes, and socks. Bending the right leg still involved some minor pain. Then he stripped off his shirt and underwear and looked up to see Mary already in bed beneath the sheets. As he turned towards her, she gasped as she saw the still livid scars on his right hip.

"It doesn't look too bad. Do you still have pain?" she said.

"Putting shoes and socks on and off and climbing a lot of stairs, those are the things that seem to trigger some discomfort. Not sharp pain, but a deep ache. But there is something much more important that I want to try and see whether that induces any problem." He sat on the side of the bed and gently lifted his lower body onto the mattress. Then he was in her arms. She squealed a little as his cold hands touched her naked flesh. "My darling Mary, how I have missed your loving warmth. Do I need to take any precautions?"

"No, no. Just take me. I want to feel your strength inside me." Colin began to raise himself to lie on Mary but as he did, he flinched with pain.

"Stop. Let me come on top," Mary said. "I can tell that was hurting you." She raised herself above him. Her breasts fell to his lips as she grasped his member and gently lowered herself. "Oh, that feels so good," she whispered. "I needed reminding." She started to move on him. "I'm not hurting you am I my darling?"

"No, with your knees are either side of me, I can barely feel your weight." Other than occasional self-stimulation, they had talked about this early in the marriage and both had agreed it could be necessary when they were separated for extended periods, they had had no sexual outlet for months. She started to grind her mons area against him and within a few seconds he spasmed and poured his seed into her. The liquid feeling deep in her vagina combined with the thrusting against him, triggered her orgasm and she squirmed and wriggled her body on top of him. He flinched a little and she immediately stopped and rolled off him.

"I'm sorry, did that hurt you? Mary asked.

"Just a little at the end when you put your full weight on me. Maybe if you did that but mostly on the left side, it would be fine. And in any event, everything will eventually strengthen up and it won't be a problem. I love you so much my darling." They lay close together enjoying the relief provided by their union.

"You seem a little distracted. I mean I understand you are still recovering from a very nasty accident and you have just got home, but something is worrying you, right?" Mary's usual intuition was working well he thought. She could read his emotions like a book.

"Yes, but first of all, tell me how my sisters are," he said trying to collect his thoughts.

"They are both fine and very busy with the hostel," Mary said.

"Hostel, what hostel?"

"Your mom and dad bought an old house in town and they are converting it to a hostel for backpackers and bicycle tourists."

"Well, that's a surprise, what on earth got them going on that?"

"Your two sisters of course. They have always been outdoorsy types haven't they. And they convinced your parents that a hostel would be a good investment in Arisaig. They plan to put advertisements in the Glasgow and Edinburgh newspapers once the house is ready. It will have a dormitory room with six single beds, and a double room for couples, so they could accommodate eight people at a time. And they are planning to offer breakfast for a small extra charge. But you are avoiding my question." Mary pulled his head towards her and stared into his eyes. When she did that, he remembered the first time he had felt himself falling into their depths.

"OK, I am worried, and I have been all the way back on the ship from Singapore. There is no way that the company will allow me back to sea. They will let me go and I will have no future in the merchant navy. What am I, and that means we, going to do?" His voice was strained.

"Colin, Colin my dear. You shouldn't be getting yourself so worked up about this right now. You need to be resting and getting your health back. You know that Douglas and Morag will always look after us until we are able to get back on our feet. Sorry, I didn't think about what I just said, but you know what I mean. You're a very smart man and if you can't stay with Blue Flags, then I'm sure you will find something else productive to do." There was silence in the bed. "Umm, did you hear what I said?" He didn't reply. She waited. She knew he was struggling with the situation. Since deciding to leave Arisaig and seek his fortunes at sea, she knew he was determined to become a Captain and probably a very senior Captain commanding the company's largest vessels. She reached up to his face and felt wetness there. Was her strong and fearless husband weeping a little? He had never cried in her presence before, and her heart melted. She hugged him tighter and whispered how much she loved him. As she did so, she could feel his erection growing and pushing against her belly. "My, my, seems like he's looking for more attention," she said.

"Let me try to come on top of you this time. Is it OK?"

"Yes my dear, my OBGYN in Fort William asked me whether I wanted to be one of the first women in the area to try the birth control pill. I said yes, so if I get pregnant, we'll blame her." He gently eased himself over her putting most of his weight on his elbows and left side. He felt a few twinges from his right hip but once fully inside her, such minor pain was forgotten with the growing desire in his loins. He started to feel Mary respond to his thrusts and her breathing quickened.

"I need to slow down otherwise you'll get me again and I want you to reach a climax first." He slowed his thrusting but pushed so that the area immediately above his penis was pushing against what he now knew to be the clitoral area. He continued slow thrusting and grinding, and he could feel her tension building.

"Yes go, go, oh that feels so good." Her words made him thrust ever more strongly and she started spasming beneath him. Within a few seconds he too reached an ecstatic climax and release as his seed, now somewhat diminished, pulsed into her. "That was so good, I want more," she said.

"I'm afraid you'll have to wait a few hours for me to recover. I know I've been away for a long time, but twice in an hour has fully depleted my supply." She laughed at his silly words, and then got out of bed and went to the bathroom. Even after two babies, she still looked wonderful from the rear, a little broader perhaps, but still beautifully shaped.

Colin had dinner at the hotel alone with his father. Morag and Mary were minding the children and having room service.

"Mary told me about the hostel," Colin said.

"Your two sisters can be very persuasive. But I think it's a good idea and investment. People are starting to earn a little more and starting to take holidays. The area between Fort William and Mallaig is scenically beautiful and attractive to those who like the outdoors. I think the hostel will do very well in the summer. It'll be quiet in the winter, but that will give us time to make repairs and such. But let's talk about your future, son." Colin was over his depression. The afternoon in bed with Mary had cleared his mind and the self-pity was gone.

"I have to believe that I'm finished at Blue Flags. I mean, they need fully fit deck officers, not men who walk slowly with a gimp." Colin's words came out a little harshly and his father looked at him with a slight smile on his face.

"Don't be so sure that Blue Flags is done with you. You may not be sea going, but Captain Thurmond indicated to me that they want to talk to you about another opportunity." His father's words stunned him. What possibly could they be thinking about? "You know the company has 32 vessels in the fleet right now with plans to expand that number over the next decade. And they are getting rid of a lot of the old stuff and introducing new vessels every year."

"But what could they want me to do?" Colin asked again.

"I don't know, but I'm sure that's why Thurmond wants to see you at 9 am, don't be late."

Captain Thurmond's office in the company's headquarters building on Water Street in the center of Liverpool, was large and beautifully furnished with an antique desk, gleaming mahogany conference table and chairs, Persian rugs, nautical prints, and a view of the city that included the Mersey river.

"Colin, how nice to see you. You are looking quite well for a man who has suffered the kind of accident that would have laid others low for a long time." Thurmond's voice carried the authority of a man who had captained many vessels and now was chief among those captaining the entire company.

"Thank you, Captain. I also want to extend my full appreciation to you and Blue Flags for covering all expenses of my accident and subsequent hospital stay and trip home."

"Least we could do. Our investigation by the way, established that it was a sling from the lighter that failed and caused the pallet to swing out of control. We've sued the lighter company but frankly we don't expect to recover anything. We won't be using them again however and that will be plenty enough damage for them."

"I figured that that was might have happened. I know our slings are always inspected before we use them, and I've discarded a few with even minor problems." There was a lull in their conversation as a middle-aged woman came into the office with a tray with coffee pot, teapot, milk sugar, spoons and cups and saucers. The china all bore the company's insignia and was identical to that used in the officer's dining room on the ships.

"How are your family managing? Your father of course is a legend in the company, and I was pleased to see him briefly yesterday. He looked very well. I understand that you have two children."

"Yes, I was thrilled to see them standing on the dock waiting for me," Colin replied. Thurmond pointed at the tray.

"Tea or coffee?"

"Coffee please." Thurmond poured them both coffee and then sat back in his chair.

"Colin, you have done very well in the company to date but I'm sure you have realized that it will be impractical to have you continue as an ocean-going officer." Thurmond looked directly at Colin who nodded. "But, when we have someone of your calibre working for the company, we are loath to have them leave. Over the last ten years the company has continued to grow and as you know, we now have 32 vessels in four different classes. That's not quite right of course, we still have the one old boat in a class by itself, she'll be retired later this year when the Paleamon gets delivered from Harland and Wolff. But it's surprising how boats, even of the same class operating on similar routes, have different cost and expense characteristics. We collect data on the cost of operation of all our vessels, but we've never done any real analysis of these figures. We plan to establish a department here at headquarters to do just that, and we would like you to head it up. The purpose of the department would of course, be to come up with ways to ultimately reduce our costs and expenses while still providing the high quality of service to our customers that the company has always prided itself on. It's getting an extremely competitive shipping world out there, and any way we can reduce our expenses and costs, will be important for us to remain a shipper of choice." There was silence in the room. Colin was at a loss for words. Was this something he wanted to do? Was it a golden opportunity or a dead-end office job? Would his family have to move to Liverpool ? These and many other questions surged into his head. He didn't know how to answer Captain Thurmond who was clearly expecting some kind of response.

"Captain, this has taken me aback. It sounds like it could be an important function for the company, but of course it would not be like being at sea. Please let me think about it for a day or two. I need to talk to my wife as, I assume, we would have to live in Liverpool."

"Of course, but you should know that this position would be the equivalent of a junior Captain and would carry an equivalent compensation package. The position may also require some travel either by ship or air. All such travel would either be in our vessels or by premium class in other company's vessels or airliners. Please give it your fullest consideration. The owners are aware of these plans and have advised me of their interest in having you run the department."

As Colin left the building, he felt almost shell shocked. On the one hand he could stay with the company he loved, get good pay and benefits, and become heavily involved with the business side of shipping. On the other, he would be in a stuffy office all day every day, he would desperately miss the open ocean, the diversity of ports and places that a voyage entailed, and the sense of independence that the crew of an ocean-going freighter developed. This was going to be a tough decision. He needed to talk to Mary. He knew already what his father would say, 'take the job, it's a great offer'.

CHAPTER 7

Tom Parker had worked for the Blue Flags Line for over fifteen years, but he had never been to sea and had decided early on in his tenure with the company, that he never wanted to. He had joined the firm straight out of grammar school and had started work at headquarters as an office boy at a salary of £7 10s a week. Tom was a diligent young man, clean shaven, dark haired, and almost handsome in a rakish sort of way, and he soon advanced to a junior clerk position where he was exposed to some of the key elements in the business of a shipping company. Now, he was a manager responsible for the acceptance of passenger bookings on all the company's vessels through communication with port agents in the vast areas plied by the ships of the Blue Flags fleet. Then he had to verify that space was available for the passenger, and that payments from said passengers had been received. He would wire or radio the pursers on each ship to identify that space was available and then to assure that all necessary visas and passports, boarding, baggage handling, cabin, dining and drinking arrangements were in place. On the wall adjacent to his desk was a large magnetic whiteboard with the name of every vessel across the top and the ports of call for those vessels on movable magnetic markers in a column beneath. Next to the ports of call was a written number representing the number of passengers planned to be on the vessel when it left that port. Previously, he had used a large chalkboard which, because of its constant use for updating, had spread chalk dust all over his workspace. The magnetic whiteboard was his idea, and one of the few that management had accepted.

As he had moved up through the ranks of the workers at headquarters, he had seen and occasionally met, senior managers and the company's owners. The only manager he liked was a man named Colin McDonald who was head of fleet operations. He had had a few interactions with him and felt that McDonald treated him as another 'crew' member and didn't in any way scorn or degrade him. The owners were a different kettle of fish. Although respectful in front of them, he found them arrogant, supercilious, and condescending. As time wore on, he gradually came to realize that he hated and distrusted them, they did not care a whit about him and in fact were disdainful of his working-class background, his lack of a university education and his disinterest in going to sea. But he envied their wealth, wealth he thought, gained off his back and the backs of many others in the office and at sea. Although he was now paid a wage that provided a modicum of disposable income, he had been able to move out of his parent's house in Aigburth and rent his own place, he coveted the ease of their lives. They didn't have to worry about unexpected bills, they drove fine cars and lived in big houses in leafy suburbs with their expensively dressed wives. He could barely afford to take his girlfriend out to dinner, and he had no idea how he would ever have enough income to marry her. Not that he had asked for her hand, she didn't interest him that much, but she was a comfort on the weekend when she would often stay in his flat on a Saturday night, cook him dinner, watch movies, often pornographic movies, and then satisfy his sexual needs.

The reservation for Jacob Bakker had come from the agent in Rotterdam. Tom recognized the name. Mr. Bakker had traveled on the Blue Flags Line several times and had just made reservations for a trip on the Olympus leaving Rotterdam in about six weeks.

"Hey Willie, we've had Bakker before, right?" Tom asked the agent on the phone.

"Yes, I have spoken with him on previous occasions. He hates to fly and always takes the ship to and from Singapore. He has a lady companion that usually goes with him and he always pays for her fare."

"The man's got to be wealthy, do you know what he does for a living, and why does he go to Singapore? I mean, if I'm not mistaken, this must be his third or fourth trip." Tom wasn't quite sure why he was asking the questions, but there was something brewing in the back of his mind that had not yet surfaced to his consciousness. "Do you know where Bakker is from and what he does for a living?" Tom asked.

"He calls me form Antwerp, but what he does, I have no idea."

"But why is he going to Singapore regularly? He seems to go there maybe once or twice a year, stay a month or so, and then come back to Liverpool. He's also going and returning with this lady, Fiona Marchbanks."

"Why are you so interested in this guy?" Willie asked.

"I don't know, just seems strange to me what the guy is doing. I mean, does he just like cruising on a Blue Flags vessel, or he is he going to Singapore for some reason?"

"Let me do some digging on this guy, maybe I can find something."

" OK, let me know what you uncover."

It took Willie two weeks to get back to Tom, but when he did, the information he had was intriguing.

"This guy Bakker is a diamond merchant. There are quite a few of them in Antwerp and he works, maybe owns, one of the more prominent firms. His company gets raw gem quality diamonds from South Africa or wherever, cuts them into various shapes and then sells them on to jewelry manufacturers. The reason he's taking the cruises is that apparently the guy is deathly afraid of flying. He goes to Singapore once or twice a year on business. Why would a guy be doing that? I figure he must be taking diamonds with him. I mean the Far East is one of the strongest markets for fine diamonds. And the lady he goes with seems to be his main, if not only, squeeze. According to my source, she's a hot number and maybe a conniving bitch, but Bakker thinks she walks on water."

"Wow, you really got the dope on this guy, who's your source?" Tom asked.

"One of his employees who ain't at all happy with what he gets paid and how he's treated."

"Join the club, that's exactly how I feel."

"Hey, that makes three of us. Would love to get my hands on some of those diamonds. Would convert them to cash and buy myself that big BMW I've always wanted." Willie was only half joking.

"Are you serious?" Tom asked.

"Err, well I mean, these rich guys don't give a fuck about us. They make all the big money, and we scrape by." Willie had a sharp edge in his voice now.

"Willie, if we somehow got hold of a shipment of diamonds, what the hell would we do to turn them into cash?"

"Wait, do you think there's any way we could get our hands on a shipment? Let me think a minute." Willie was quiet.

"Willie, are you still there?" Tom spoke into the phone not expecting a reply.

"Yes, I'm still here. You got me thinking Tom. I mean if I could find how Bakker carries the diamonds, could you do something on the ship?"

"My cousin is a third mate with Blue Flags. He's as pissed off with them as I am, and he's scheduled to sail on the Olympus. That's the vessel Mr. Bakker will use on his next trip to Singapore."

Tom met his cousin David Parker in a pub on Rice Street in the center of Liverpool. Ye Cracke, better known as The Crack, was a 19th century pub. One of its claims to fame was that John Lennon and his girlfriend Cynthia, often visited the pub when they were at art school in Liverpool. Tom and David sat in a barroom whose walls were covered with pictures of Liverpool from the last 100 years. The room had that distinctive spirits and beer odour, and the walls were yellowed with countless years of being exposed to cigarette smoke. David was four years older than Tom and should by that time, have risen to a higher position in the Blue Flags Line than that of third mate. But his attitude towards the company and his willingness or lack thereof, to go along with whatever his superiors wanted of him, had held him back.

"Dave, I got an idea, but to make it work I need your help," Tom said. Dave was on his third pint and was feeling pretty loose.

"What the fuck are you talking about lad?"

"Dave, listen to me, if we could make this work, we could all get a lot of money and quit this stinking company." Suddenly, Dave seemed to sober up.

"Tom, you got my full attention."

"There's going to be a passenger on the Olympus who I believe will be carrying a slew of diamonds. Is there some way we can snatch that shipment, and convert it to cash in a hurry?"

"Jesus Tom, are you crazy? How do you know this guy will have a bunch of diamonds with him?"

"Never mind how I know. Is there some way we could lift those diamonds?"

"Well, maybe, but as soon as we lifted them the guy would know, and we'd be fucked because they would search the ship and find them."

"Not if he didn't realize that they had been stolen."

"You're losing me man, what are you talking about?"

"Don't worry about that right now, just tell me if you could get into his cabin or maybe the ship's safe if that's where he keeps them."

"The safe would be more difficult but not impossible. I'd need some bribe money though. And how would I get off the ship with the loot."

"Through our agent in Penang, I can arrange for a fishing boat to go out into the Malacca Strait and meet the Olympus. I can get a special package for you to put the diamond bag in and then drop overboard. The fishing boat will take it to shore for you to pick up." Tom looked enquiringly at his cousin who was rolling his eyes.

"Jesus, you ain't asking for much are you. How much would we have to pay the fisherman?" David asked.

"Haven't closed that deal yet, but what do you think? You want me to fill you in on the plan," Tom said. David sat looking at his cousin. He seemed very serious about the idea; it wasn't the beer talking.

"OK, shoot."

CHAPTER 8

When his cousin had first described the scheme to David at the pub in Liverpool, it sounded crazy. But the more they talked, and the more he thought about it, he began to realize that it just might work and even sharing the loot, he would still be a rich man. Willie had told Tom that his contact at the Bakker firm wanted a big cut, but he was a key to the whole plot. The Bakker employee, known only as Karel, had told Willie that the value of the next shipment would be worth close to US$4,000,000. He also told Willie that he could get a velvet bag from the company storeroom, get it filled with worthless little pebbles, and then sealed using the company's wax and impression. The bag would exactly duplicate the actual diamond bag shipment used by Jacob Bakker. He had also indicated how best the real diamonds could be fenced for hard cash in Kuala Lumpur or Singapore. He told Willie that they could expect to get maybe US$2,500,000 from the sale and he wanted no less than US$700,000 for setting the whole thing up. He was risking his job and his freedom to participate in the heist, and he knew that he, as a Bakker employee, would be investigated, so once he got his money, he would not be able to start throwing it around. He would have to wait a few months and then quit the company purportedly for a better job elsewhere.

But when it came to his part in putting the plan into action, David was having second thoughts. If he got caught, his life would be shattered, he would wind up in a British jail and when he got out, he would have few if any friends and would never be able to get a decent job. And what would happen to his cousin and the other two guys in on the scheme? Could he hold out against the police interrogation or would he give up the others. But he was unhappy with his job at Blue Flags, he hated the four on eight off watch hours and the three to four-month voyages that made it difficult to maintain a relationship at home. He had been married, but his wife had soon tired of his sea going absences, and they had divorced only fifteen months after the wedding. Fortunately, there were no children. He had had girlfriends since the breakup, but he never seemed to be able to keep them. No, he wanted out of the merchant navy and the money would allow him to start a new life, maybe buy a small business somewhere, meet a sweet sexy girl and settle down, even have a family.

He thought long and hard about how best to access a passenger's cabin on the ship without anyone being aware. He had decided that he needed a cabin master key. He knew from experience that the three stewards who serviced the seven passenger cabins, there were five double cabins and two single cabins, each had a pass key good for all seven. One steward was always on call, and two others cleaned and serviced the cabins during the day or early evening. But he realized that if he asked a steward for the key, that in any ultimate investigation that fact would come out and he would become a prime suspect in the theft of the diamonds. No, he had to get a master key for himself without anyone on the ship knowing about it. He knew that there was a board on the wall of the Purser's office where keys were hung for various rooms and storage areas. The board also included a rung for a cabin master key. All the keys were normally in a locked glass cabinet which enclosed the board. The Purser held the key to the cabinet but often left the cabinet unlocked particularly when they were in port and loading provisions. As the Olympus rounded the Cape of Good Hope and headed for Durban, David had devised a plan where he would replace the master key with his own cabin key, take the master key ashore, get it duplicated, then return the original master key to the cabinet and retrieve his cabin key. The Purser was always busy when they were in port and David's only concern would be that he would lock the glass cabinet when he left his office to attend to some provisioning matter. But David figured that even in that worst case, he could pick the lock. He had been practicing this latter skill since leaving the UK, where before leaving he had purchased some literature and some picks from a back-street shop in Liverpool.

As it happened, the Purser had carelessly left the glass cabinet open. The master key had a small piece of red tape stuck to it, and he peeled this off and stuck it on his room key before putting the room key on the master key ring in the box. He went ashore and got the key duplicated at a store that sold everything from toilet paper to power washing machines. His plan had worked perfectly until he got back on the ship. As he entered the office, he found the Purser seated and working a hand operated adding machine.

"Hey Dave, what can I do for you?" the Purser asked as he looked up from his accounting task. David had to think fast, he had not expected this complication.

"Errr, Bill, I'm sorry but I've mislaid my cabin key. Bloody stupid of me I know. You got a spare here? I may have left the key in the dining room or somewhere. I know I used it to lock my cabin as I came out, but damned if I can find it now."

"Not a problem, why don't you borrow the master key. Bring it back to me as soon as you find your own cabin key. If you never find it, we'll get you a new key, but we'll have to change your lock to do that." The Purser got up from his office chair, went over to the glass cabinet, unlocked it, and gave David the key from the master key ring. As David climbed up the stairs to the officer's cabin deck, he smiled to himself. In about half an hour he would return to the Pursers office and give him the master key. The key the Purser had handed to him was of course his own cabin key that he had hung there before going ashore.

CHAPTER 9

"Ladies and gentlemen, thank you for your patience." All the passengers were seated in the ship's main dining room along with the deck officers. A bar had been set up at one end of the room and stewards were waiting to provide service. The passengers had been contacted individually by the first mate and requested to attend an important meeting with the Captain. They all knew that something had gone wrong with the ship as they were moving very slowly, and sails appeared to have been set at three points on the ship. The Captain's voice was calm, but serious.

"As you are all aware, there has been an accident on the ship. About six hours ago, there was an explosion in the engine room that has disabled our main propulsion power unit. Tragically one man lost his life, and another has been seriously injured." There was a gasp from a few of the passengers. "All of our engineering officers and staff are working as hard as they can to repair the damage, but I have to tell you that it is significant. The Chief Engineer will be reporting to me later today on the situation. If the damage to our main engine can be repaired, it will be, and we will proceed on to Penang and Singapore where the ship will be taken out of service. If the damage cannot be repaired, we will have to radio for an ocean-going tugboat, and we will have to be towed to the nearest major port. Our position at this time, is approximately 1000 miles northeast of Madagascar and 1,500 miles southwest of Ceylon, sorry, I believe that nation very recently became Sri Lanka. So, in this latter circumstance, it will be twelve or more days before we would reach port. I apologize on behalf of the Blue Flags Line, for this disruption to your travel schedules. I have been in radio contact with our fleet operations department, and they are fully aware of our situation and will act accordingly once the Chief Engineer has reported to me. I realize this may come as a shock to you all. It certainly was for me too, but I want to assure you that we are in no danger. Are there any questions?"

"Who was killed and injured?" The woman's voice was faltering, and she appeared close to tears.

"The man who died was a technician commonly termed an 'oiler'. He was of Pakistani descent. The third engineer, who was in-charge of the watch at the time of the explosion, was burned and concussed, but he's being treated in our sick bay and we believe will survive. If we were closer to a port, I would ask for a helicopter to come and take him to a hospital better equipped to deal with his injuries. But we are out of range of that kind of aircraft." The Captain answered the question while looking directly at the woman who was now openly crying.

"If the engine can be repaired, when do you estimate, we could get going again?" The Captain had anticipated this question, but the questioner, a dark-haired man, Mr. Lovett the Captain recalled, appeared agitated and even angry.

"Mr. Lovett, until I speak to the Chief Engineer, I cannot answer your question. However, from my limited experience of this kind of situation, if the main diesel engine is repairable, I would guess that we could be underway in three or four days," the Captain said.

"This is damned inconvenient. I have important meetings in Singapore that I am going to have to reschedule. Once we know the situation can I send a message to my people in Malaya?" Lovett's selfish and inconsiderate tone appeared to shock some of the other passengers.

"Of course, anyone that needs to communicate with persons ashore, will be able to do so. Now, if there are no other questions, I would like to offer you all drinks on the house, please ask the stewards for whatever you would like. We have champagne, vintage red and white wines, English and Belgian beer, and of course all spirits."

Mr. Lovett was not the only one who was angry at the situation they found themselves in. Third mate David Parker, who had been sitting quietly in the back of the room, realized he had a major problem if his cousin's scheme was going to work out.

CHAPTER 10

I had never seen such destruction. In the confined space of the engine room, the explosion and fire had, besides the death and injury, caused significant damage. The fuel feed system and compressed air starting system on one of the diesel generators had been wrecked and the spilled fuel had fed the fire for several hours. Various pipes and valves had been ruptured and smashed, floor plates and railings twisted in the heat, lighting smashed, electrical wiring and insulation burnt and severed, air vents and ducts shredded, and the telegraph system to the bridge disabled. There was detritus on all the horizonal surfaces and piled into the bilges at each the side of the space. There was a major cleanup and repair job ahead of us. Fortunately, the main switchboard was in a separate protected area in the engine room and electrical power to the rest of the ship had been maintained.

But the biggest issue was the main propulsion engine, without which, we were subject to the whims of Indian Ocean currents and weather. To provide a minimum of steerage way, the Captain had ordered the very unusual setting of sails. I had never appreciated that a modern cargo vessel could have sails, and up on deck the sight of three canvas expanses streaming from the derricks used to lift cargo to and from the holds, was a rare sight. But at least the ship could be kept facing the long ocean swells rather than being broadside on and rolling severely from side to side. I realized later that it would have been nigh on impossible to repair the main engine if we had been subject to the constant rolling action of the swells. It took over three days to get the engine repaired and get the ship underway again. I developed a great admiration for the Chief Engineer, he had clearly been through this before and new precisely what had to be done in the long sequence of removing massive engine parts, repairing them or replacing them with spares, and then reassembling them into a working engine. Some of these parts weighed four or five tons and were difficult to maneuver in the close confines of the engine room. In many cases there was only one way to get a particular piece in and out of the engine, but the chief knew exactly how to position the overhead crane, tackle, winches, and cables necessary. Being young and inexperienced cadets, there was little we could do to help the process, but we watched and learned. We also spent days cleaning up the mess and helping with repairs to pipes, valves, and electrical systems.

Later in the voyage, I came to realize that the accident and the ensuing delay to the ship's schedule, precipitated a sequence of events that almost cost me my life.

CHAPTER 11

"Thank god we've got going again," Fiona said. "Not sure how much longer I could have put up with that delay and the ship's motions."

"My dear, other than jumping overboard, I'm not sure you could do anything but grin and bear it." Jacob's words were meant in jest, but Fiona turned to him with a half sneer on her face. "And it seemed to me my dear that you brought a lot more clothes with you on this trip."

"I think you enjoy these trips more than I. They are just so long, and I thought I might cheer myself up a little if I wore a larger selection of outfits, particularly when we get to Singapore. I have read almost all the books I brought with me and the ship's library seems to be limited to rather lightweight novels and such. Besides eating, drinking, and sunbathing, what else is there to do?"

"Well, we have been doing some other, very pleasant things." Jacob smiled at her and grabbed her hand to kiss it.

"Oh Jacob, sometimes I think you have only one thing on your mind," Fiona said. In fact, she had become bored with their lovemaking months earlier. Jacob had a certain way of going about things that he never altered. He never instigated an impromptu encounter. It was always in bed and always followed the same routine. This and other aspects of his character had started to grate on her nerves, and she knew she would soon have to leave him. Although he had been good to her financially, she rarely paid for anything when they were together, her overall monetary situation since the divorce had deteriorated more than she had anticipated. She had spent a good deal on furnishing her Kensington apartment, she had bought a new car, an MGB sports model, and she had completely redone her wardrobe including hats, coats, suits, dresses, evening gowns, underwear, lingerie and shoes, a lot of shoes. She had also had some work done on her face and chin. She was thirty-five, and some lines and wrinkles had started to show. She was still a beautiful woman, but her vanity had dictated that she get the cosmetic surgery and she was happy with the results. But all of these had cost money.

On the last trip over six months ago, she had decided that she would change her life one way or another. Either she would become a wealthy woman of the world, with a new name and living in Australia and maybe California, or she would be in prison. She had never thought of herself as a criminal person, but at her age, she knew she could not continue relying on men who, after having sex with her quickly disappeared, or men, such as Jacob, who she eventually tired of and could no longer tolerate. She had left school at age eighteen and started a modeling career that worked well for a while. But the constant sexual attention of men, and the need to satisfy them to get ahead, had soured her on the business. So now, she had no skills to fall back on, no career to continue, and no intention of taking a low paying menial job somewhere. No, she had decided that she would steal Jacob's bag of diamonds on the next trip they would take together to Singapore.

Once she had made the decision, it was as if her mind became solely focused on the accomplishment of the theft and her planned subsequent disappearance. She made nice with Jacob, even though she was finding that harder and harder to do. Often, during their lovemaking she would think of some other man she had enjoyed earlier in her life, there had been quite a few. This allowed her to feel more passionate even if Jacob was oftentimes inadequate. But as they had journeyed on towards Singapore, when Jacob was out of the cabin, she opened his suitcase with a duplicate set of keys. She had bought him the suitcase as a Christmas gift. It was hand-made with a solid leather body and she had urged him to discard the rather old and worn suitcase he had been using. At the time she had purchased the case, she had retained the second set of keys solely because she thought that made more sense if he somehow lost his set. But as her plan developed, she realized that Jacob had no idea she had them and that the duplicate set would now come in very handy. So, she took the opportunity to carefully examine the black velvet bag that contained the diamonds. With her quick shot camera, she took many pictures of the bag and the bag sealing method. She measured the bag and noted its width, height, and thickness. She hefted the bag to estimate its weight. It was very light, much less than a pound, probably only a few ounces. The stones felt loose inside the bag, she could push them around from the outside and it seemed like there were over a hundred in the bag, all different sizes. She could find no brand name or other identifying mark on the bag but of course she couldn't open it to find if there was a label inside. Further, she could not tell whether the bag was lined but she didn't think that mattered. The velvet was of high quality and a dense black color. The closing mechanism was a draw string of black silk like material that was pulled together at the top of the bag and sealed with heavy red wax impressed with the company seal which included the name 'Bakker'. She knew that Jacob did not open the bag until he was in his agent's office in Singapore. She carefully restored the bag to its position, closed and locked the suitcase.

She also started to think about all the things she must do before the next trip which she figured would be in about six to eight months. Her first and most important action would be to find someone who could make a bag identical to the one Jacob used, to part fill the bag with tiny worthless stones, and to close and seal it exactly as she guessed the Bakkar factory would do. She had to assume he would carry the stones in precisely the same way he always had. He was very much a creature of habit, so why would he change the method he used so successfully? The pictures she had taken would be important in duplicating the bag and closure. She went to a clothing store on Bond Street and asked to see the head seamstress. She had purchased a lot of clothing at the store, and they were happy to serve her in any way they could. She asked the seamstress whether there was a private room they could use.

"Does madam wish to have some measurements taken for a new dress or suit," the seamstress asked deferentially as she closed the door on a dressing room. She was a small woman with almost black hair turning to grey and in her black dress, she looked like an old grandmother. Her hands appeared almost gnarled, but Fiona guessed that she must have strong fingers to be sewing all day.

"No, no. I have a special secret assignment that I would like you to undertake for me. If it's possible, I will pay you personally rather than through the store," Fiona said. The seamstress looked abashed and hesitated.

"I'm not sure I can do that madam, but what do you have in mind?'

"My boyfriend has asked for my hand in marriage. I love him dearly and I want to get him a special engagement present. I know he's getting me one. I have bought him an antique backgammon set and I'm having the checkers specially made from ivory. I want a velvet bag to put the checkers in. I have pictures here of what I want it to look like." Fiona pulled her camera from her purse and started to show the seamstress the pictures she had taken on the ship.

"I can make something exactly like that for you madam including the silk closure tie, but I can't seal it like the one in the picture."

"That's fine, don't worry about the sealing. The velvet must be deep black in color and of the finest quality. I have written down the exact size I need." Fiona handed the seamstress a piece of paper with the bag's dimensions written on it. "How much would this cost, between you and me?" The seamstress appeared sheepish.

"I could work this up for you for £50, madam. If you wish to pay me directly, I will purchase the material myself and do the work at home. I have all the equipment I would need there. I would not want to do anything here in the shop, it wouldn't be right."

"I understand perfectly. Please go ahead." Fiona handed her a £20 note and a card showing her name and phone number. "I think it would be good if I saw the material before you made the bag. Would that be possible? Could you call me and perhaps we could meet at Fortnum and Mason for tea, and I could look at what you've got?"

"Of course, madam, that would be very nice."

Her next project was to get a new passport in the name of Felicity Montcrief. One of her former boyfriends in London, a hot lover but a decidedly shady character, would help her with that. She knew it would cost her, but it had to be done. She had chosen the name because she liked it and because it matched her current initials on certain of her luggage and jewelry items. She would also get credit cards in her new name. She would open a bank account in the Cayman Islands and then one in Sydney, Australia in her new name, and then transfer whatever funds she had from her London accounts to the Caymans and then Sydney before closing them. She would apply for credit cards in her new name using her Cayman account for credit. There was some risk in this, but she felt she had to have active credit cards to carry out her plan. Finally, she would need to secretly sell her apartment and her new car, it only had 3,000 miles on it, and plan for whatever she received from those sales to also be transferred. Then she would close the Cayman accounts. She believed that with the secrecy accompanying accounts in that island nation, the ultimate destination of her funds could not be traced. She also started to plan on what she would tell her friends. She realized that once the police and insurance investigation began, she would become a prime suspect and she needed to provide as much misdirection as she could. She also worried about how she should turn the diamonds into cash. If she tried to sell them all at one time, and she no idea how to do that, she felt that that would likely draw the attention of the police. No, she provisionally decided that she would sell a few stones at a time at various cities in Australia and North America.

CHAPTER 12

David Parker had the counterfeit bag in his possession and, once he had duplicated the master passenger cabin room key, had been waiting for an opportune time to substitute it for the real thing. The contact at Bakker had sent the bag directly to him at his Liverpool home address. Bakker must be keeping the real bag in his cabin because he had not requested use of the ship's safe. Once he got the real bag and the Olympus entered the Malacca Straight, David would look for a fishing boat which by day would be flying a distinctive red and white flag and by night would flash a red signal every 30 seconds. Tom had got the name and phone number of the fisherman from the company's agent in Penang. He told the agent that a prospective passenger was interested in a fishing trip and the agent recommended Sagari Megat and gave Tom his contact number. David had argued at length with his cousin about using the fishing boat. Why couldn't he just keep the jewel bag and hide it on the ship. And why did they each have to come up with £300 to pay a half share of the fisherman's fee? But Tom had insisted that the jewel bag be got off the ship as soon as possible after David had stolen it. He reasoned that Bakker could check on the bag's contents at any time and if he discovered the robbery, a major search of the ship would take place and the bag eventually found.

When Tom had spoken with Megat, he had told him that his boat must appear to be fishing. Once the fishing boat had been spotted, Parker would toss the diamond bag overboard in a waterproof container that would initially submerge. Tom had bought the device from a ship's chandler in Liverpool. After about half an hour, and with the Olympus almost ten miles away, sea water would dissolve a capsule that would in turn inflate a float that would take the container to the surface. The float had both a radio homing device and a small green light, both of which were also activated by seawater. They would be used by the fishing boat Captain to retrieve the container and bring it to shore. Then in Penang, David would meet with Megat, pay him the £600 fee he had agreed to, and take possession of the container with the diamond bag inside. There was risk that somehow Megat would double cross him, and he had thought about how he would cope with that. Once he had the bag, he would discard the container and then call the Majestic Hotel in Singapore and make a reservation for two days hence. Then he would go to the local DHL store, put the diamond bag in an express package and send it to himself to be held for his arrival at the Majestic. In Singapore, he would go to the hotel, pick up the package, cancel his reservation and contact the name that Tom had provided to him. The fence was supposed to be reliable and safe to use, but this was undoubtedly another risky part of the plan. If all went well, he would get paid the total fenced value in cash. He had been told that the payment would be either in 100 US Dollar bills or 100 Swiss Franc bills.

He had figured that either way the cash would weigh over 70 pounds and he planned to take a large rucksack ashore. He had also planned to immediately return to the ship and stash the rucksack in his personal locker. Then, later that evening, he would move it to an area of the forecastle that was dark and difficult to access. Once he got the cash back to the UK, the plan was that he and Tom would both get approximately US$800,000, Willie would get US$100,000 and the contact at Bakker $700,000. They had told Willie and his contact that they would have to come to Liverpool to get the cash.

Back in his berth, David Parker started to sweat. How long was the ship going to be stuck here in the middle of nowhere? The accident and delay had thrown a real wrench into the works. Parker had found out from the steward who serviced their cabin, that Mr. Bakker had two large and one small suitcase in the closet and that the two large cases were unlocked, and the small case was always locked. Parker had asked whether there were unusual items left around the cabin, but the Filipino steward said he had seen nothing out of the ordinary. Parker figured that the diamond bag was in the small, locked suitcase and that he would need 15 minutes uninterrupted in the cabin to pick the locks, substitute the fake bag for the real one, relock the suitcase, and get back to his berth. And how was he going to get a message to the fisherman in Penang without it being noticed? If he were unable to communicate with the shore, the guy would be out there on his boat waiting for the Olympus to come over the horizon. And when she didn't show up on time, how much patience would he have, how long would he stay out in the ocean waiting for the vessel? Also, with the removal of the Olympus from service in Singapore, he realized that he would have to keep the rucksack in his possession until he knew what his personal situation was going to be. And he knew that once Mr. Bakker found that his bag was full of worthless stones, he would demand that the company search the ship and that everyone who had been on the ship would come under suspicion. He decided that once he had the cash, he would put the rucksack in a storage locker at the central bus station until he knew where he was to be sent.

CHAPTER 13

The repair work in the engine room continued day and night. The Chief Engineer had informed the Captain that the main engine could be put back in service in perhaps three days, but that the ship could then proceed only at a much-reduced speed, probable 9 to 10 knots versus the normal 16 to 18. I continued to be amazed at how the engineering officers, oilers and other technicians worked. We two cadets did all we could to help, but we went to sleep for seven hours at night while the others seemed to work on. There was little that we could do as concerning the main engine, but we were able to help with repairing wiring, piping, valves, and vents. It was extremely hot in the engine room even with the ventilation fans going full blast once we got them back into service. On the evening of the third day after the explosion, we closed the crankcase, and attempted to turn over the big diesel engine using the compressed air system. All fingers in the engine room were crossed, because if the new and repaired parts did not work properly together, we would hear it immediately. The opposing pistons in the eight cylinders moved up and down and the massive crankshaft rotated. One major concern was that the explosion had somehow bent or distorted the crankshaft. No evidence of that had been uncovered, but you never knew until the engine turned. We heard no untoward noise, and the compressed air was shut off and the engine stilled. The crankcase doors were removed and the crankshaft and the many bearings linking the connecting rods to it, examined with portable lights. No damage or distortion to the bearings could be seen. The Chief Engineer, who by this time looked haggard, dirty with oil and grease, and desperately in need of some sleep, ordered the engine to be started. The supercharging blowers were switched on, and once again the compressed air was fed into the cylinders to start the engine turning. Then vaporized diesel fuel was injected and the combustion process commenced. The engine gradually built-up speed as more fuel was injected. The Chief Engineer was on the ships phone to the bridge advising that we would attempt to maintain 50 revolutions per minute. The engine was solidly coupled to the single large propeller that drove the vessel and we soon started to feel the familiar motion of a ship moving through the ocean swells. It was all smiles down there next to the big engine. The engineering crew had worked long and hard for this moment and they all hoped that the repair work they had done would be sufficient to get us to Singapore. I felt elated too, although I had had little to do with the real work. But I had witnessed what engineering skill, experience and perseverance can accomplish, because when I first went into the engine room after the explosion, I thought that there was no way the vessel was going to move under its own power again.

At the reduced speed we were told that it would take the ship approximately twelve days to get to Penang. This was six days longer than scheduled and with the three-day repair period, meant we would reach there nine days late.

"Gentlemen, I want to thank you all for your work in repairing the damage from the explosion." The Chief Engineer had the entire engineering staff, except for three personnel on watch below, assembled in the dining room. "I am glad to tell you that third engineer Jimmy Preston is improving. He'll have some nasty scars but otherwise he'll be fine. As you all know, Hamza Malik lost his life. The company will return his body to his family in Karachi and will also provide two years pay as compensation to the family." There were murmurs of approval from the other Pakistanis in the room. "I personally have only experienced one other crankcase explosion accident, and it was a lot less severe than we experienced. I have had to do several major main diesel engine repairs at sea. It's never an easy job and as you know we have had to do a lot of patchwork. We have been running for a day at 50 revolutions and I am going to advise the Captain that at 1400 hours today I want to stop and once again examine the crankshaft, connecting rod bearings and other engine parts. This is just a precautionary measure, no one has reported hearing anything untoward, but if any part of the engine is under abnormal stress, we ought to be able to see, feel or smell it. If that inspection reveals no problems, we will restart and go to 70 revolutions. We will make our stop at Penang and then at Singapore, the Olympus will be taken out of service. I don't need to tell you what a big deal that is. We'll have to unload all cargo and except for a skeleton unit, the entire crew will be ashore until a replacement ship is available. To my knowledge this has only happened three times in the company's recent history. Olympus may go into dry dock in Singapore and significant work will be done to get her back into good shape. Right now, it looks like Triton will come up from Perth and load the cargo. Some of us, but probably not all, will board Triton as supplementary crew. Others will be flown to ports in Asia to board company vessels or will be flown home. That's about all I can tell you at the moment. Any questions?"

"Yes chief. Shouldn't there be some kind of device inside the crankcase that can sample the atmosphere and sound an alarm if a dangerous oil mist develops and the temperature starts rising," the second engineer asked.

"Good one Alex, invent such a device that can work in a foolproof manner, and you might make some money," the Chief Engineer responded.

"Chief, how long do you estimate we will have to wait for Triton?" my fellow cadet asked.

"She's already been notified, and she should be leaving Perth tomorrow. It'll take her six to seven days to reach Singapore, so she'll probably be there before us. She's a steam ship, so some of us here would not have the necessary experience for work in her engine room."

CHAPTER 14

Fiona had substituted her velvet bag for the real diamond bag while the Olympus was headed south through the Gulf of Guinea off the west coast of Africa. Jacob had left the cabin for his morning constitutional walk around the vessel. He said he made twenty circuits which normally took him over an hour, so she felt she had plenty of time. She was most careful not to move the small leather suitcase in any way as she gently opened it with the duplicate key. When she held the real diamond bag in her hand, she realized that the velvet felt different from her fake bag but that otherwise, the fake bag and closure looked exactly like the real bag. She didn't think that Jacob would notice the difference in the velvet, he normally wouldn't handle the bag until they got to Singapore anyway, he just looked in the suitcase to make sure it was still there and intact. She hid the real diamond bag in a zippered cosmetic case that she kept in a draw in the bathroom adjacent to their bedroom. She was confident that Jacob would never go looking through her stuff, particularly her cosmetics. At some point she would break the seal and open the bag just to look at and feel the diamonds, but she decided to wait until later to do that. She felt elated, all her plans to date had worked out. But the delay in the Indian Ocean and now the slow progress of the ship towards Penang and Singapore, had left her uneasy. What if Jacob decided to check on the jewel bag? If a thorough search of the ship was conducted, would she be able to keep the real bag somehow hidden? She eventually calmed herself, she knew Jacob well. There was no reason for him to go beyond his normal visual check of the bag. It was critically important to him and the agent in Singapore, that the seal be unbroken.

She started to fantasize about her new life as a wealthy widow for she figured that was how she would project herself once she reached Sydney. She imagined some new handsome man wooing her and desperately wanting to bed her. She imagined dressing up and going to the theatre with him and then to dinner in a fine restaurant. She imagined his tongue exploring her mouth as they stood on the balcony of her hotel room overlooking the lights of the city.

"A penny for your thoughts my dear." Jacob's voice shattered her reverie.

"Oh, I was just thinking how long this trip is taking."

"Yes, I'm sorry about that. I have never been delayed like this before, a first time for everything I guess." Jacob's placid acceptance of their situation annoyed her. He was so calm and middle of the road about everything. She wondered if that would change when he opened the bag and found a bunch of small pebbles. She would love to be a fly on the wall in that room. She thought he might finally show some emotion. She knew the diamond shipment was insured, he would lose some money with their loss, but he would survive. But she didn't really care anymore about how he felt. It was becoming more and more difficult to live with him every day and to lie in bed and suffer his predictable attempts to arouse her.

"Jacob, I think I will go and visit some friends in Hong Kong and Japan rather than travel back to Europe on another ship." She could see by the fleeting expression on his face that in fact her words had shocked him, but he recovered quickly.

"Well OK, if you must. I know you are starting to find these long sea trips tiresome." So, he was beginning to sense her frustration, she would have to work a little harder the next few days, make him feel he was still wanted. "How and when will you get back to London?" he asked.

"Not really sure how long, maybe three or four weeks. Then I'll fly back, probably on BOAC. I'll write to you regularly, so you'll know what I'm doing." The lies were easy and followed the pattern of misdirection she had started with her friends in London.

"I think they are changing their name to British Airways and they have that big new plane the Boeing 747," Jacob said.

"For someone who will not fly, you seem to know a lot about airlines," Fiona said.

"Well, I read about them in the newspapers we took on board in Durban," Jacob responded.

"Maybe I'll be able to fly on one of the new planes, that would be interesting. More room than the 707, I would hope. I think that when we go ashore in Penang, I will make a reservation to Hong Kong."

"Who do you know there?" he asked.

"A friend from school, she's married to a British Government official. I think I'll probably stay with her." She didn't want to use a name.

"Have you been there before?"

"No, but I understand it's an amazing place."

"Yes," he responded. "But don't look out the window as you are landing at Kai Tak Airport. On a voyage a few years ago, a fellow passenger told me that you can literally see people hanging their washing out of the window of high-rise apartment buildings right alongside the flight path. It unnerved him. Where does your friend live?" She had to think quickly, what could she remember about Hong Kong from geography classes in grammar school. "I have her address somewhere; I think it's on Victoria."

"You will enjoy your time there I'm sure, send me postcards with your letters. I won't get them until I get home to Antwerp which could be after you get back to London. It takes over four weeks on the ship and I will take the train from Liverpool to London and to Harwich and the ferry to the Hook of Holland."

"Of course, my dear, but I'm not planning on rushing home," she said as she thought that she would likely never return to London.

As the ship plodded northeast across the Indian Ocean, she and Jacob returned to their normal routine. One morning when he was out walking around the vessel, she unzippered her cosmetic bag and stared at the black velvet. Should she break the seal? She felt the diamonds through the fabric, there seemed to be more than she had expected. But if she did break the seal, how would she make sure that the bag stayed closed? Would the silk string keep the bag tightly shut? She decided not to break the seal, and she returned the diamond bag to her cosmetic case.

CHAPTER 15

David Parker had decided that he must get a message to the fishing boat Captain. The fishing boat had certainly been out there looking for the Olympus already. He figured that the only way to do this without drawing too much attention, would be to send a message to the company's agent in Penang. He went to the radio room.

"Hello Freddie, can you get a message to the agent in Penang for me," David asked.

"Sure, but what's the problem? He knows we're going to be nine days behind schedule," Freddie responded while looking enquiringly at third mate Parker.

"Last time I was in Penang, I went fishing and I promised the fishing boat Captain that when I was next in the area, we would go out again. I need to let him know, through the agent who knows him, that we are going to be late."

"OK not a problem. What's the message?" Freddie said.

"The message should read 'Arriving Penang nine days later than scheduled, please advise Megat'."

"That's all?"

"Yea, that should be sufficient. Thanks." Parker left the radio room and crossed his fingers as he returned to his cabin. He didn't know what else he could do. They were about five days from entering the Malacca Strait and he knew he had to get into the Bakkar cabin tomorrow or the next day at the latest.

Taking the diamond bag proved easier than he expected. While the Bakkar guy and his girlfriend were at dinner he entered their cabin using his duplicate master key. He was able to pick the lock on the suitcase in three minutes, it was a decent lock but easy to pick. He had practiced on his own suitcases. He lifted the lid and there was the bag. He lifted it out and held it in his right hand while he pulled the duplicate bag out of his pocket with his left hand. Everything seemed the same, size, weight, color, closure, and sealing, but somehow the bags were not the same. The black velvet felt different, the bag from the suitcase felt a little rougher. Whatever, maybe the diamond company had a new batch of bags or something. He substituted his bag, pocketed the bag from the suitcase, carefully closed and locked the suitcase and left the cabin. As he was exiting the cabin, he noticed one of the engineer cadets walking towards him along the companionway.

"What are you doing up here, Marlin isn't it?" Parker spoke sharply, the cadets were not supposed to be up there, particularly in their boiler suits.

"Sorry Mr. Parker, I am taking a message from the engineer on watch to the Chief. He didn't want to wake the Chief by calling him on the ship's phone, so he asked me to push the message under the Chief's cabin door."

"OK but get on with it and then get off this deck." With these words Parker turned away and disappeared down the corridor.

Four days later, the Olympus entered the Malacca Strait headed towards the port area for Penang. Parker was on the four to eight watch and had seen nothing from the bridge. After getting a quick snack, he was out on deck by 9 pm scanning the horizon. The night was dark, no moon yet, and the sky was a panoply of stars. There was a faint glow from the ships running lights, red on the port side and green on the starboard and he could see a very faint light behind the bridge windows. This was the second night he had been looking for the signal from the fishing boat. At about 0100, he thought he saw a light on the horizon on the port side. It could just be a star rising, but no, it was red, and it flashed briefly ever thirty or so seconds. This was it, his heart leapt, the message had got through and the pick-up boat was there. He went to his cabin and opened a porthole preparing to throw the container out into the ocean, but he stopped. He wasn't sure that the package would drop completely clear of the ship. The last thing he needed was the package to be sucked into the ship's massive propeller which would shred it to pieces and send the diamonds to the bottom of the ocean. So, he checked the companionway outside of his cabin, then slipped out again onto the deck carrying the container and worked his way up to the forecastle area of the vessel. He looked back up at the bridge where the officer of the watch would be stationed. It would be difficult if not impossible for him to be seen from the bridge as he had donned dark clothing before exiting his cabin. Hiding behind a stanchion, he threw the container with all his might into the air, it sailed on the wind for a moment and then plunged into the ocean where the bow wave of the ship pushed it away from the hull before it sank out of site.

CHAPTER 16

Fiona thought Penang was hot, smelly, and dirty. She and Jacob had taken a cab from the pier into the city and to what they had been told was the best hotel in Georgetown. As they entered the lobby, a blast of cool air surrounded them, the hotel had air conditioning. She was wearing a light summer dress, a beautiful silky fabric with a neckline that showed off her bust to full advantage.

"Oh my god, that feels so good," she said. Their cabin on the ship had ventilation but no air-conditioning and traversing the Indian Ocean had been unpleasantly hot. "Maybe you should try to find a shipping company that has air-conditioned cabins."

"I did and none of the cargo companies do. There is a Swedish line that says that a new vessel soon to be launched will have such amenities, but I'm not sure it would be on the Europe to Singapore route," Jacob said. "Anyway, let's get a drink." He realized that Fiona was becoming less and less enthused with the long sea trip. Perhaps this was the last time she would do this with him. That would be a shame, because although she could whine and moan about the environment, he had grown to rely on her company even to the point of believing that he was in love with her. She was a beautiful woman and it always pleased him when men's heads turned to her when she entered a room. The bar at the hotel was no exception and as they settled on stools at the highly polished wooden counter, all male eyes were on her. He also knew that she relished the attention, that she was vain and somewhat selfish, but she was his.

"I think I'll check with the hotel's concierge about making my flight reservation to Hong Kong. When will we get to Singapore and are we going to stay at Raffles again?" she asked.

"I think we should get there by Sunday night, that would be June 11th. Yes, we will stay at Raffles of course, you like it there, don't you?" Raffles was a venerable and famous hotel. The rooms were comfortable and the food and drink, excellent.

"Yes, yes, I like the hotel, it has a wonderful ambiance. But I think I'll make a flight reservation for Thursday June 15. Why don't you go to the restaurant and get us a table for lunch while I talk to the concierge." She didn't ask him whether that would be acceptable. She clearly was determined to go on her own way, and he knew it would be fruitless to argue with her. After she had spoken to the concierge about flights from Singapore to Australia, she actually made no reservations, they had lunch at the hotel before walking around the town. They needed to get back to the ship by 5 pm as the Olympus was due to sail at 6.

As Jacob Bakkar and Fiona Marshbanks were lunching, David Parker was at the fishing dock trying to find Sagari Megat. Once ashore, Parker had called Megat's number. A woman had answered. Her English was poor but eventually Parker had learned that Megat was on his boat, and that the boat had no name, simply a number, B227. It was hot, humid, and stinky on the fishing dock, and there must have been forty or more ramshackle vessels tied up at even more ramshackle piers. It appeared that many of the boats housed families with kids bouncing around half naked, barking dogs and Malay women cooking on makeshift stoves. He was growing frustrated in his search and with £600 in his pocket, the less time he spent in the dock area the better. Eventually he found B227, and it appeared deserted, but as he approached, a wizened older man emerged from the single covered cabin area. The boat seemed to be in better shape than many of the other vessels and certainly more suitable for taking tourists out on fishing trips.

"Are you Mr. Megat?" Parker asked.

"Mr. Parker?" His English was halting.

"Do you have something for me?" Parker asked. The man waved at him to come aboard the fishing vessel. The stench of rotting fish was almost overpowering and did not improve as Parker descended into the small, covered cabin.

"I spent much time in the Strait waiting for you," Megat said.

"Yes, I'm sorry. But you did get my message?"

"Yes, but I still was out there for almost two days. What do you have for me?" Megat's tone was almost threatening.

"Show me the container." Parker wanted confirmation of the pick-up. Megat reached behind him and pulled the container out of a dirty sack.

"Is this want you want?" The container appeared to be intact, but Parker wanted to open it and check that the bag of diamonds had not been tampered with. He grabbed the container and ripped the closure apart before Megat could stop him. Megat stood up, he had a small knife in his hand. Parker held his hand out. He was sweating profusely.

"No, no Mr. Megat, there is no need for that. I have your money, but I need to check inside first." He thrust his hand into the container and found the black velvet bag with the closure still sealed. Megat still held the knife and by the look on his face, Parker was convinced he would use it if the money weren't exchanged immediately. He pulled the roll of bills from his jacket pocket and thrust it at Megat who sat, put the knife between his knees, unrolled the banknotes and started to count them.

"It's all there Mr. Megat, £600 as was agreed." Parker stood to leave. Megat picked up the knife again.

"What is so valuable in the bag?" Megat's words were hard to understand but his intent was clear. Parker backed away and drew a small handgun from his inside pocket.

"We had a deal Mr. Megat. You have your money and I have my bag. I'm leaving now. I never want to hear from or see you again. And if you want tourists referred to you for fishing trips, you will never speak to anyone about the pick-up and my visit here. Do you understand?" Megat looked at the gun and put down his knife. As Parker left, Megat spat and muttered words that Parker did not understand. Once back on the dock, Parker moved quickly away from the fishing boat. He was shaking as he repocketed the gun and stuffed the velvet bag in his jacket pocket keeping the used container in his hand. He had no ammunition for the gun and had thought twice about bringing it ashore with him. But he had known that this was one of the riskier parts of the plan. As he walked further away from the boat, he tossed the weapon and the empty container into the filthy dock water.

At the street entrance to the dock, he got a cab to the town center. He located a store that handled DHL shipments and bought a small shipping box. He withdrew the diamond bag from his pocket and held it for a moment. The seal was still in place but when he looked closer at it, the word Bakker impressed into the red wax, didn't look professional. It looked like it had been done by hand. Whatever, the diamond company must have had some problem with the sealing device. He placed the diamond bag in the package and addressed it to himself at the Majestic Hotel in Singapore. With a black marker he added the words 'Hold for Arrival of Guest' below the address. After paying for the shipment, he used the phone in the store to call the Majestic Hotel in Singapore and made a reservation for Sunday and Monday June 11 and 12. He then went to the nearest bar, rapidly drank his way through three San Miguel beers, and finally started to unwind. So far, the plan was working.

CHAPTER 17

The McDonald family's move from Arisaig to Liverpool had not been easy. Mary was both upset at having to leave her teaching job and concerned about what it would take for her to get credentialed in England. On top of that was the radical change in the two children's lives. They were used to the remote small-town nature of their home, and to be thrust into the hubbub of a big city, with traffic and noise and new schools, was a cultural shock. Even though they missed their friends, they were both young enough that it didn't take long for new friendships to form. In fact, their new home was not in Liverpool but across the Mersey in the Wirral, an upscale residential area where in fact they were somewhat insulated from city life. Colin and Mary had soon focused their house hunting on the Wirral area as that seemed to be what Mary wanted. They eventually bought a two story four-bedroom house in Bebington, and Colin purchased a three-year old Humber Hawk saloon car for his commute to and from the Blue Flags office in the city of Liverpool. Mary missed her in-laws and friends in Arisaig and Mallaig, and her parents in Edinburgh, but she had Colin at home every evening and for two days on most weekends, and that made up for the losses.

McDonald's stature within Blue Flags had steadily grown. He soon became a key figure in the company's management, and when Captain Thurmond retired in 1966, he took over his position as chief of fleet operations. His initial assignment analyzing company cost and expense data by vessel had led to numerous improvements in the way the company-controlled expenditures. It also led to the dismissal and ultimate jailing of several pursers and a couple of senior deck and engineering officers. The data analysis found that certain pursers often seemed to spend more on food, drink and other provisions, or their vessels always seemed to be short on supplies. When a specific individual had been so identified, Colin would fly out to meet the ship at a foreign port and would perform a snap audit of the purchases made by the purser versus what actually had been taken on board. In most cases these audits turned up false invoices or shortages on provisions that should have been on-board. Often, under questioning the offending purser would confess, in an attempt to minimize whatever punishment, he might be subject to. In most cases, Colin worked with the vessel's Captain to bring the purser home under lock down conditions, and then once back in the UK, the individual would be taken into custody and tried in a British court. Colin never lost a case although he did lose a few pursers who found out Colin was coming, fled the ship before he arrived on board, and disappeared into the foreign country. He would notify the local police of the man's identity, but it was rare for any of these individuals to be caught.

A more significant issue was the apparent discrepancies between fuel usage on ships of the same class on similar routes. Because fuel consumption would increase dramatically if a ship operated at maximum speed, the company's policy was to operate all modern motor ships at about 16 knots and modern steamships at 17 to 18 knots. Most vessels would bunker, or take on heavy fuel oil, once during a round trip voyage. Before the Suez Canal had closed in 1967, this bunkering was normally done at Aden, where fuel could be purchased at the minimum world price. But after closure of the canal, unless the vessel had cargo for, or to pick up at, Djibouti or Aden, the bunkering was done at Durban in South Africa or at Singapore. Many tons of fuel were loaded and the opportunity for criminal manipulation of invoices or actually boarded quantities, was always present. It took at least two officers to accept delivery documents and to verify quantities taken on board. Thus, a minor conspiracy would be required to get a kick back from an onshore oil supplier who delivered 1000 tons but invoiced and was paid for 1200 tons. Colin uncovered two such cases in the 1962 to 1966 period and both appeared to have been going on for many months. One case involved the rare occurrence of both the Captain, Chief Engineer and two other officers systematically defrauding Blue Flags. The investigation revealed that over an eighteen-month period, the four men had in total, received £60,000 in kickbacks from the oil supplier. How the money was split between the four men was never determined, but all four served extended jail terms.

When he became chief of fleet operations, Colin combined the data analysis function into the department and appointed a new department head. This allowed him to reduce his travel schedule and focus on how best to deploy the fleet in meeting the needs of existing and new customers recruited by the marketing division. He also became responsible for developing the basic specifications for new vessels as the company's fleet slowly expanded. This was a critical part of his job. The new vessels represented a very significant investment for the company, and when they came into service the boats had better be efficient, cost effective, and fully capable of meeting the needs of the company's customers. Thus, many of the determinations that fleet operations developed were subject to scrutiny throughout top management and Colin often found himself presenting and justifying his findings to the company's owners. He was also responsible, through a separate department, for the crew rostering for all vessels, crew training particularly as such related to the new vessels, and for the recruitment of new deck and engineering officers.

His duties also included the direct support of ships that encountered trouble in one form or another. Trouble included accidents of all types and difficulties with shore authorities, shippers, tugboat companies, and believe it or not, pirates. Whenever a ship collided with a dock, collided with another vessel of any size, ran aground, or ran against rocks, suffered damage in a storm or worse, foundered in a storm, suffered damage loading or onloading cargo, or suffered damage from a fire or explosion on board, Colin was to be immediately notified so that fleet operations could map out a plan for recovering, repairing, or resolving the situation. The news of the crank case explosion on the Olympus on Thursday May 25, 1972, was received in Liverpool about three hours after it had happened. This was a serious accident at a distant location in the Indian Ocean and Colin realized at once that the vessel would probably have to be taken out of service at the next port where reliable repair services where available. He had communicated with Captain Mosgrave who had told him of the death of one man and the injury to another and that the Chief Engineer was assessing the situation after having put out the ensuing fire in the engine room. Colin thought about dispatching emergency medical services and an oceangoing tug to assist the Olympus and if necessary, tow her to port. But her position was so far from any port and the difficulties of accessing and then towing a 10,000-ton cargo vessel in the heavy swells of the Indian Ocean, made the notion of providing emergency services in any quick manner and a towing operation, very tenuous. In addition, such an operation would be expensive and disruptive to the shipping schedule for the cargo. The nearest Blue Flags vessel was over 1,000 nautical miles northeast of the Olympus's position and could not reach her in less than two and a half days. No, he decided to wait for Captain Mosgrave to let him know the extent of the man's injuries and whether repairs could be made by the engineering crew. He notified his staff in Singapore of the situation and the need to take the Olympus out of service when and if she was able to get there. This would require other company ships to take on and deliver her cargo. He also tentatively had himself booked on a flight from Heathrow to Singapore leaving on Friday June 9th. He wanted to personally visit with the injured man, the third engineer, and inspect the vessel before authorizing repair work sufficient to get her back in service and back to the UK where the company could make whatever other repairs were necessary.

Twenty-four hours later he heard from Mosgrave that although the man had been burnt and concussed, they could deal with the injuries on the vessel. Mosgrave also advised that the chief and engineering crew were hard at work on main engine and other repairs and that if successful, they could be underway in about forty-eight hours. This was all good news. Two days later Colin was informed that the Olympus was headed for Malaysia but at a reduced speed and was now scheduled to arrive at Singapore on Sunday June 11th. He confirmed his booking on BOAC.

It was late in the evening when Mary asked him how long he would be gone for. Her words had a note of complaint he thought, as he continued to read that day's Liverpool Echo. "I have become so used to having you with me," she said.

"I think it will be at least a week my dear. I thought that if I'm going as far as Singapore, I should go up to Hong Kong for a day to talk to the Port Authority. They want to move our terminal and it will be quite disruptive to our operations there. We need to come to terms on some kind of arrangement, both monetarily and with the provision of a new terminal before we have to leave the old one." He said this while continuing to stare at the newspaper. She screwed up her face at him.

"Oh, come on, it isn't that bad," he said. Mary looked away. She didn't want to get into an argument, she hated herself when that happened, and it seemed that it was happening more frequently these days. Colin seemed so absorbed in his work, and with Joan away at college, he barely ever spent time with John. Why was that? John was his son, but it always seemed to Mary that Joan was his favorite. And their lovemaking had grown less and less frequent. It was as if Colin was wedded to his work and not to her. She decided that now was as a good a time as any to tell him how difficult it had been for her when he was at sea. She would steer clear of the other issues for the time being.

"I don't think, my dear, that you ever have understood how much I missed you when you were gone for months at a time. Not just your physical presence, but knowing that if any problems came up, and they did frequently, you would be there to help me with them." Her words snapped his concentration and he swung in his chair to look at her.

"What do you mean? You never said this before." His tone was sharp, too sharp. "Sorry, I am a little shocked by what you just said," he felt flustered. "You mean that you suffered every time I went on a voyage?"

"Of course I did. But I wanted to be the willing and compliant wife. I didn't want to put you under any pressure or guilt. I knew you loved the sea. I did not want to take that away from you." He got up and came over to her and pulled her up from her chair and put his arms around her. "That's why I didn't put up any resistance to the move down here. I was so happy to know that I would have you at home most of the time." He looked into her eyes and saw the beginning of tears.

"Oh Mary. And you held these feelings in for over ten years." Now she was weeping, and her tears soaked into his shirt. Except for her gentle sobbing, they stood quietly hugging each other.

"I was never worried about leaving you. You have always seemed so capable and unflappable. And all that time I was away, you were miserable. How did I miss that?"

"Because once you were back with me for a few weeks, I was so happy," she replied. "And when I knew you had to leave again, I would hide my worries and concerns. I have become so used to having you home, I guess this impending trip just set me off. I'm sorry."

"Don't be sorry, I'm the one who should be sorry. Let's go to bed." It was the first time in many weeks that they had made love. She felt the old passions rising as he caressed her, kissing her throat, her breasts, the inside of her thighs and then her sex. He pulled her on top of him, and as he slid into her, she began to rock back and forth, building her pleasure slowly. He didn't reach orgasm as quickly these days and it felt wonderful to feel his hard member against the walls of her vagina, as she ground her clitoral area into him. As the orgasmic spasm shook her, she cried out and dug her nails into the flesh of his upper arms. That seemed to trigger his response and his seed surged into her. They lay, exhausted by the lovemaking and the emotions leading up to it. They separated but remained close together, shoulder to shoulder, hand in hand.

"You know that Joan had met a boy over in Mossley Hill", she said.

"I seem to remember something about it, wasn't that a year or so ago?" he answered.

"Yes. Well, I found out that he was a cadet on one of your company's courses at the technical college, Riversdale I think it's called."

"Oh yes, must be an engineer type then, we don't have any deck trainees over there."

"I feel a bit guilty because I told her not to get serious about him. She was upset with me. I think she quite liked him. Anyway, she told me she had dumped him. I shouldn't have interfered, but I didn't want her to wind up in the same situation I had had for almost fifteen years." Colin remained silent for a while.

"I really did not comprehend that my time away was such a strain on you. How come you can read my emotions so easily and I totally missed something so important in you?"

"Difference between men and women and particularly between you and me, I suppose," she answered.

"Well, I should only be away for a week or so this time, I'll soon be back."

Early Friday morning, the company car pulled up outside ready to take Colin to Manchester airport from where he would fly to Heathrow for his connection to Singapore. As Mary waved goodbye to him from their front door, she had a sudden cold and chilling feeling, almost a foreboding. But she quickly ignored it. He would call her from London and when he got to Singapore.

CHAPTER 18

The Olympus, still operating at about two thirds of her normal cruising speed, reached Singapore late on Sunday night June 11. When Jacob went out on deck Monday morning, the activity around the ship was frenetic. Cargo was being unloaded simultaneously from all the holds, lowered to pallets on the dock and then immediately moved by noisy fume belching fork-lift trucks. It was clear that all the cargo was being removed for loading onto other company vessels. He looked down the dock and saw another Blue Flags ship immediately astern of them. He read the name on the ship's prow, Triton. It appeared that much of the cargo coming off Olympus was going directly to Triton. He figured that the accident had been an expensive event for the company, but he was impressed with how the aftermath was being dealt with now that they were at Singapore.

They had been advised by the first mate that they would need to disembark the ship by 12 noon on Monday, and he and Fiona had packed all their bags the night before. He had checked the small suitcases contents one more time before retiring and had found everything in order. He had an appointment to meet with his agent at 9 am on Tuesday morning, and the two of them would go over the inventory of all the stones to verify that everything was in order. On the many trips he had made, there had never been a problem. Then on Tuesday afternoon and Wednesday, he and Fiona would do some sightseeing and shopping. She had insisted that she would take a cab on her own to the airport early Thursday morning.

"I think I'll take a leisurely walk around the grounds and the hotel shops," Fiona announced once they reached Raffles and settled into their room.

"I'll come with you my dear," Jacob responded.

"No, I would prefer to go on my own, besides which I know you don't really enjoy traipsing around shops with me."

"OK, but don't be too long, you know how I enjoy a little time in bed with you in the late afternoon." Fiona almost grimaced at his words but she recovered quickly, smiled at him sweetly and said she would look forward to it. As she left the room, she figured that when she did return, it would probably be the last time they made love and she could cope with that.

Once out of the room, Fiona went immediately to the hotel concierge who made a first-class reservation for her on a Malaysia-Singapore Airlines flight to Sydney, Australia leaving at 0900 on Thursday June 15th and eventually arriving in Sydney at 2220 the same day. She also had the concierge book her a single room at a Raffles sister hotel in downtown Sydney for three nights with guaranteed late arrival on the Thursday. She used the name Felicity Montcrief for both reservations.

"They plan to change the airline's name," the concierge said. "All the international flights are going to become Singapore Airlines later this year. I think the plane will be a Boeing 707, although they will soon be introducing the big 747. You can pick up the ticket at the airline counter when you check in."

"That's fine. I will pay for the ticket at the counter. Thank you for your help." She left the concierge desk and went to the bar where she bought herself a gin and tonic charging it to their room. The drink calmed her. She was nervous about the likely events of the next few days. She had deceived friends and lovers before, but only in a small way. She had never undertaken a deception that if it went wrong, would have her wind up in jail. As soon as Jacob opened the velvet bag, all hell would break loose. Would he suspect her? Would the police get involved and try to stop her leaving Singapore? She had thought long and hard about this both in London before she left, and during the sea trip to Singapore. She knew she could not simply disappear as soon as reaching Singapore. That would make her a principal suspect and she had purposely delayed her fictitious trip to Hong Kong so that she would be with Jacob after he found out that the diamonds had been stolen. She knew she had to be to terribly upset for him, but not go too far and exhibit a 'she exclaims too much' demeanour. She had hidden the velvet bag in the toe of one of her day dress shoes and she had stuffed that and the other shoe of the pair with tissue paper. Then she had put the pair in a shoe bag and buried the bag in the suitcase she used for carrying all her shoes. She doubted that anyone would demand to search all her belongings, but she wasn't completely sure how Jacob would react. She finished her drink and went out to the shopping plaza in the hotel. She decided she would buy him a little keepsake, he needed to keep believing she was very fond of, even loved, him. She found a pair of gold cufflinks that she knew he would covet, and she bought them using a Fiona Marshbanks credit card. As she signed the sales slip, she thought that that was probably the last time she would ever use the card. She intended to cut up and dispose of all her old cards at the first possibly time after she left Singapore.

She also wondered if she should try to suggest to Jacob what might have happened to the diamonds. If she did, she would point to his company in Antwerp and infer that someone there must have made a switch before he had left for the trip. To her knowledge, he hadn't opened the bag since he had left his office. The wax seal was still in place. But perhaps he had sealed the bag himself, she didn't know. In any event, she knew he would get over the loss of the gems. How he would ultimately react to losing her, she couldn't predict. She didn't feel a need to hurt him, but she knew she had to leave him, not just because she had stolen his company's assets, but because she could no longer tolerate being with him. It was a shame, but she recognized that this had been a pattern throughout her life. Perhaps she was incapable of really loving a man to the point of wanting to spend her life with him. But she had never had a yen for a relationship with a female. She had lesbian friends in London, and she had been unable to understand how such women enjoyed love and sex with each other. She was not critical of such relationships; she just couldn't relate to them.

When she got back to their hotel room, Jacob was already in bed. The noise of her entry had woken him from a light sleep, and he smiled broadly.

"My darling, you look gorgeous. What have you been doing?" he asked. She sat on the side of the bed, leant over, and kissed his cheek.

"I have a little something for you my dear," she said as she handed him her purchase. He brought his hands out from under the sheets and opened the package.

"Oh, these are beautiful, thank you so much. What have I done to deserve such a nice gift? I will wear them tonight to dinner." He held her hands and pulled them to his chest. She knew what he wanted, and she got up from the bed and went to the bathroom. In just a minute she returned to the bed naked and slid in beside him.

CHAPTER 19

Colin McDonald arrived in Singapore at 6.15 on Saturday evening. It was an exceptionally long flight from London with four stops, Zurich, Beirut, Karachi, and Calcutta, along the way. He felt sluggish and tired as he went through customs and was happy to see a driver holding a Blue Flags card, waiting for him at the Arrivals concourse. The heat and humidity hit him as he walked out of the terminal to the waiting car. He was taken directly to the Majestic Hotel where after checking in and taking a shower, he had a light dinner and went to bed. He woke at some strange hour in the night, jet lag was working as usual, and he could not get back to sleep. He looked at the bedside alarm clock, 3.45 am. What time was it at home? His quick calculation said 8.45 pm Saturday evening. He called Mary. The connection was way better than he had remembered from the time of his accident in 1961, and although there was some delay on the line, they were able to converse. She sounded upbeat and happy, and it set his mind at rest. Ever since their conversation four days previous, he had been wondering if somehow, he had let her down, taken her for granted. Did she still love him? He certainly loved her. He had never looked seriously at another woman since their marriage. He had realized that he must pay more attention to nurturing their relationship. He had been so focused on work, he had to spend more time with her and Joan and John. After the call, he tried to go back to sleep and eventually, after reading the hotel's in-house magazine, he drifted off. The Olympus was expected to arrive Sunday evening, and in the morning, he went out for a walk in the city. He soon realized that it was too hot for exercise and he returned to the hotel where he spent the rest of the day relaxing and preparing himself for the week ahead.

At 9 pm he was watching television in his room when the phone rang.

"Captain McDonald, this is Tony Mosgrave."

"Hello Tony, glad you made it. Must have had been a little tough out there with no propulsion."

"We were fortunate we didn't lose house power. First time we set the sails in my career. But kept our stem into the wind and cut down on the rolling," Mosgrave said.

"How's Jimmy Preston doing?" Colin asked.

"He's on his way to the hospital right now. Some nasty burns, but he should make a full recovery except he'll have some bad scars on his neck and back."

"I'd like to inspect the ship with you first thing in the morning. Would like to have Chief Robinson with us. How's he managed all this?"

"He's dead tired, but he did a great job. We would have to have been towed in without his expertise and hard work."

"OK, I'll meet you on the dock at 0800. And please let me know when I can visit Preston in the hospital."

Colin was amazed at the repair work, much of it temporary, that the engineering crew had performed. It was clear that a major explosion had occurred, and that serious damage had been done.

"Chief, how on earth did you get the main engine back in operation?" Colin asked as Captain Mosgrave stared around the engine room. He had not been down there since the explosion.

"Not easy Mr. McDonald, but fortunately we still had power, so the lifting of the heavy engine parts was not back braking, just bloody awkward. My fear was that the explosion had bent or distorted the main crankshaft. If that had have happened, the Olympus would have been a dead duck. We would have to have been towed by a salvage tug and I'm not sure you would have wanted to fix her up afterwards. Might have been cheaper just to scrap her." The Chief's words struck Colin as excessive, but on quick reflection, he realized they were probably accurate.

"What are we going to have to do to get her back in service," Colin asked.

"Well, you can see that all this patchwork needs to be redone in permanent fashion. But I think the biggest problem may be that we have been taking on some water since the accident. Nothing the bilge pumps couldn't handle, but we may have sprung a plate or something on the keel. Some of the explosive force was certainly directed downward from the crankcase. I'm afraid she will need to have her bottom looked at closely and maybe even go into drydock." Colin winced at the Chief's words. Drydocking a vessel was a very expensive proposition.

"And the main engine needs checking out thoroughly. It got us here, but at 70 revolutions, not the normal 90. I didn't want to push our luck. I think you should get the Sulzer people here and have them go over every part with a fine-tooth comb. They'll soon tell us if there is any permanent damage and if so, whether it can be fixed."

"OK Chief. Let me have your written report and recommendations as soon as you can. Thank you for all you have done here. It is a remarkable achievement. I'll be visiting Jimmy Preston in the hospital as soon as they'll let me."

"Jimmy's a good lad, I've talked with him at length in the sick bay. He'll recover and he wants to stay at sea believe it or not." As the Chief spoke, Colin thought he might just have a tear in his eye. "And poor Hamza Malik, the oiler who copped it. We are in the process of returning his body to his family in Karachi and I promised them two years pay as compensation."

"Sounds appropriate. How was he killed?" Colin asked.

"Crankcase door smashed into his body and that together with severe burns, were too much for him I'm afraid," the Chief said.

"Is there anything else we should do for the family?" Mosgrave asked.

"I will arrange for a special letter to be sent to the family from the company owners. Not much else we can do but they may appreciate receiving some recognition. "I'll need their address and I assume the letter should be in Urdu. Please get that for me and confirm, Captain." Mosgrave nodded at Colin's request. As they left the ship, Colin realized he would have to make some significant scheduling adjustments. The Triton was loading almost all the Olympus's cargo, there were a few loads that would have to be picked up by other company ships. But with one less ship in the fleet, the Olympus in his mind was going to be out of service for four to six months, he needed to think quickly about how to meet their customers shipping needs without significant disruption. Perhaps they could lease a vessel from another company.

CHAPTER 20

Fiona got the call from Jacob at 10.20 am Tuesday morning.

"You are not going to believe this," he said. His voice was strained and halting. "I am shaking, I am dumfounded, this has never happened to me before."

"What my dear, what has happened, are you hurt, you don't sound well," she replied.

"When the agent opened the velvet bag, there was nothing but tiny pebbles and dust."

"I'm sorry, I'm not understanding. Where are the diamonds?" She tried to sound incredulous.

"They are gone. Somehow, somewhere, someone stole the gems out of the bag. I don't understand how that could have happened because the wax seal was intact. You can't open the bag without breaking the seal and the seal has the company's impression in it. I am totally at a loss to figure out how this has happened. I am shocked, it will be a big loss to the company if I can't recover the diamonds."

"Jacob this is terrible. Have you told the Captain? Have you contacted the police?" She continued to inject stress into her voice.

"Yes, I have done both. The Captain was dumfounded and at least as shocked as I am. He plans to allow the police to search all the crew and the ship."

"Where are you now?"

"I'm at the central police station. I have spoken with the police commissioner who has pledged to do all he can to help find the gems and the thief or thieves. Based upon what I told him, he thinks someone had access to our cabin, but when I mentioned how the bag was sealed, he just shook his head." Jacob's voice was still unsteady.

"If there's nothing else you can do, please come back to the hotel so that we can be together." Fiona felt genuinely sorry for the emotional stress that Jacob was under and somehow, the fact that she had caused it, did not disturb her.

They were sitting together at the small table in their room. It was just after 1 pm on Tuesday and in the last three hours, Jacob's world had been turned upside down.

"I have to call my partner in Antwerp as soon as it gets light there. They are seven hours behind us, so I'll call him in about an hour. He's going to have a fit. He has often chided me for making the trip and has suggested we courier shipments out by air. I'm sure he will now insist on it."

"Darling, this is not your fault," Fiona said. "And don't you have insurance anyway?"

"Yes, but only for about half of the shipments value. It will be a serious hit for the Bakkar Company."

"Have you thought about how this could possibly have happened?" Fiona asked the question as quietly as she could, she did want to get him as riled up and shaking as he had been when he first came back to the room.

"I am pretty much at a loss. Every time I think it must have been someone on the ship, I come back to the bag's closure. It was sealed just as it was in Antwerp at the factory. If the bag had been tampered with on the ship, the seal would have to have been broken. If the diamonds had been removed without breaking the seal, there would have had to be a cut in the fabric, or a hole in a seam. But the bag was perfectly intact." Fiona was quiet for a moment. She knew that her bag and seal, although an excellent imitation of the genuine bag and closure, were not exactly correct particularly the word 'Bakkar' on the seal. That had had to be done by hand. But Jacob had not mentioned any discrepancy with the bag or seal. Was he so distraught that he hadn't checked the bag carefully? And what about the agent, didn't he notice some slight differences?

"What does your agent think?" Fiona asked.

"Well Bernard wasn't there. Because of a commitment in Shanghai and our late arrival, he couldn't be in the office and his assistant, Louis, actually opened the bag. Louis had never done that before, and he almost fell from his seat when the pebbles and dust fell from the bag." Fiona breathed an internal sigh of relief, the stars were aligned in her favor, she thought.

"But could someone have done something back at the factory in Antwerp?" she said.

"That's what I'm going to get Philip started on when I call him. It's the only plausible explanation I can come up with, and even it is hard to comprehend. Once the diamonds are placed in the bag and the bag sealed, it's virtually never out of my possession. But I am going to get the Antwerp police on to the case. They will have to check the factory and interview all the employees."

"What are the police doing here?" Fiona asked.

"They are going to search all the baggage and belongings of the entire crew. As you know, most of the crew are off the ship in a hotel."

"No, I didn't know that. Why?"

"Well, I think they are taking the Olympus out of service and assigning the crew to other company vessels, but I guess that takes a few days and they have them in a hotel in the meantime. Then the police plan to search the ship from stem to stern and they have asked the Captain to provide four crew members to help with that. The chance of randomly selected crew members all somehow being involved in stealing the gems, is completely remote. So, I think the police are going about the investigation in a very thorough manner. I doubt they'll find anything though."

Fiona was poised to ask Jacob another question, and she knew there was some slight hazard in it, but that in overall terms, it would reduce the possibility that anyone would suspect her in the loss of the diamonds.

"What about the other passengers, do you think one of them might somehow be involved?"

"You know I hadn't thought about that. It's possible I suppose but they are probably dispersed to the four winds by now, I mean we've been in Singapore for three days. And how could it be one of them with the bag being untouched?"

Perhaps Jacob wouldn't even suggest that the police try to track down all the passengers. She realized that within a couple of weeks of her leaving on the fictitious trip to Hong Kong, Jacob would start to wonder why she hadn't been in contact with him and that sooner or later, when he was unable to communicate with her or find out where she was, she would become a suspect. But she would be long gone and hopefully untraceable by that time.

"Should I postpone my trip up to Hong Kong for a few days? I hate to leave you with all this mess."

"No, I thought about that my dear. You can't help with the investigation and I'm probably better off if I just concentrate on it myself. No, you go ahead."

CHAPTER 21

On this trip, I had not gone ashore in Penang. On my second voyage, I had got horribly drunk on the local beer at a bar in Georgetown. I was sick for almost two days. So, I had decided this visit to stay on the Olympus, read a book, rest, and relax. My fellow cadets had other ideas and goaded me before they left to go ashore. I wondered where I would be sent once we got to Singapore. Maybe they would just transfer me to Triton, that would be the obvious thing and much less expensive to the company than flying me back to the UK or to some other location and some other ship. The Triton was a steamship, quite a different engine room from the Olympus. The main propulsion power was derived from superheated steam generated in an oil burning boiler. The high-pressure high temperature steam was fed into a turbine which, through a massive gearbox, rotated the long shaft that turned the single propeller. Auxiliary electrical power for the vessel would be derived both from a separate steam generator at sea and diesel engines when the boilers were fired down in port. I had not yet been on a steamship, so continuing the voyage on the Triton would be interesting. We were only going to be in Penang for a day and should reach Singapore a day or so after we sailed. Since we had made the repairs and then checked the big diesel, we had operated at 70 revolutions per minute and all the temporary fixes had held up. But it was clear that once the Olympus was taken out of service, it would be quite a while before she would be ready for sea again.

When we reached Singapore, the Chief told us that we would all temporarily stay in a hotel near the port area. I would be sharing a room with John Grange. The Chief said that we would all get reassignments within a few days. But on the Tuesday afternoon we were all summoned to a conference room in the hotel. We were told that Captain Mosgrave wanted to talk to us on an urgent matter, but no one seemed to have any idea what the meeting was going to be about. As we walked into the conference room, it was clear that the entire ship's company was going to be in attendance. Even the skeleton crew that was going to stay on Olympus, were present.

"Gentleman, I have asked for this meeting to advise you of a very serious issue that has arisen." The Captain looked sombre and even a little shocked, I thought. "One of the passengers who boarded the Olympus at Rotterdam, has had a very valuable article of his luggage stolen. Although he has not yet alleged anything, he has asked that the entire ship be searched including the possessions and baggage of all crew members. I cannot overstate the gravity of this matter. The Singapore Police Department is directly involved and will be conducting the search. I want your complete cooperation with those making the search. The search will commence later this afternoon and will continue until completed. Any questions?"

"Captain, what is the nature of the missing article?" The question came from the First Mate who clearly was as surprised at this situation as us all.

"When you meet with the police, they will advise you of what they are looking for. That is all I can tell you."

"Captain, can you tell us which passenger has reported the loss." The question came from the Purser.

"I am not at liberty to identify the passenger in question." The Captain appeared flustered by this question. He clearly knew who it was but someone, may be the passenger or the police, had told him not to disclose the name. "If there are no more questions, I will ask the First Mate and Chief Engineer to take their crew members to the two adjacent conference rooms where members of the police department are waiting. Thank you." As soon as the Captain had finished, the room erupted into quiet but intense conversation. What the hell was this all about? David Parker kept to himself at the back of the room. He had had no chance yet to visit the Majestic Hotel and pick up his package. He thanked his lucky stars for that, and realized that when he did pick it up, he would put it in his rucksack, call the fence and go directly to see him to get the cash. Tom had been right about keeping the diamond bag off the ship.

I was herded, along with the rest of the engineering crew into an adjacent conference room where two Singapore police officers in full uniform were waiting.

"Good afternoon gentleman," one of the two officers said once we were all in the room and the doors had been closed. "I understand that the Captain has briefed you on our need to undertake a search of your possessions including all baggage. After that has been completed, we will be making a complete search of your quarters and all the cabins, common areas and engineering spaces on the Olympus. Mr. Robinson, please designate two individuals to assist us in the search of the ship." The police officer, who was clearly the senior of the two, had excellent English and spoke with authority.

"Sir, before I pick the two individuals, may I ask what we are looking for," Mr. Robinson, the Chief, asked. The two officers looked at each other.

"We are not able to identify specifically what has been stolen or misplaced at this time. Suffice it to say that we are looking for items in a small bag, box, or other container. The bag, box or container could be paper, cardboard, plastic, wood, metal, or fabric of some kind. So, now I would ask all of you to return to your rooms in the hotel and wait there until such time as one of our officers, contacts you. Please unpack and layout all your luggage on the beds and table. Please empty all your pockets. I apologize, but you will be patted down and if necessary, strip searched. If such a search is required, it will take place privately in the bathroom area of your room. All areas of your rooms will be searched. You will not be allowed to leave your rooms until the search has been completed and I have been informed of the results. Anyone who attempts to leave his room before I have authorized it, will immediately be considered a suspect." A collective moan went up from the crew. We were all finding this hard to believe.

"John, you look very flustered, why is your face so red? Are you OK?" We were back in our room and starting to unpack our baggage. We had both expected to be assigned to the Triton at any moment and had not unpacked our kit after leaving the Olympus.

"Phil, I'm in trouble." He was shaking and quite upset.

"Don't tell me you know something about whatever it is that's missing," I said.

"No, it's not that. I errr, got some pot while we were in Penang. If these cops find it, they'll throw me in jail. You know how crazy strict they are in Singapore." Now I understood why there had been, on occasion, a strange odor in our living quarters on the ship. I was very naive about drugs and I didn't really know what pot being smoked smelled like.

"Jesus John. Get rid of the stuff now. Flush it down the toilet."

"But I paid a bunch to get it." He almost whined in response.

"Look, it also reflects on me if you get found with this stuff in your possession. Give it to me and I'll dump it." He went to a drawer in the nightstand at the side of the bed and pulled out a dirty plastic packet half full of the weed. He reluctantly gave it to me, and I immediately went to the bathroom and flushed the contents and after smelling it, the bag, down the toilet. Never mind that the bag was likely to clog something up somewhere, we had to get rid of the odor.

"Now come in here and wash your hands thoroughly otherwise the cops are going to smell something on you." Twenty minutes later there was a knock on our door, and when I opened it two cops came directly in and asked us to stand against the wall by the door. They frisked us quite thoroughly, particularly around the genitals and rear. Then they asked us to remain standing while they went through our stuff with a fine-tooth comb. They looked at and inside everything. They checked our luggage for secret compartments. They then searched the bedroom and bathroom again leaving no stone unturned. Every cupboard was turned out. They pulled the sheets back off the beds and dumped them on the floor. They looked under the mattresses and the beds, behind the curtains, inside the closet, under the sinks and in the toilet tank. As they left, they told us to stay in the room until we received a call indicating we were free to leave.

"They would have for sure found that pot," I said.

"But what the hell are they actually looking for?" John exclaimed. "I mean they are going to a lot of trouble with this search and for such a small thing. What can be so valuable and so small?"

"Well, it's not money. It must be jewels or something," I answered.

"And who is the passenger? If I remember we had four get on at Birkenhead and then another eight at Rotterdam, right?" I thought about his question.

"Maybe one of the ladies lost some jewels. That good looking blonde had a couple of flashy rings and necklaces that she wore at various times on the trip. Maybe she got ripped off or something by one of the stewards who cleaned her cabin."

"Could be," John replied. "When we get out of here, I want to ask Fred or Tim what happened in their meeting." Fred James and Tim Long were the two deck midshipmen that we shared our ship's quarters with. "And I wonder what the cops are doing about the other passengers. Maybe one of them is a crook and stole the stuff." His comment stunned me, but he was quite right, the other passengers should be treated just the same way we were, but I somehow doubted that that was happening.

CHAPTER 22

David Parker had endured the search of his person, belongings and hotel room and had been advised that he was free to leave the room. He was starting to realize that the delay in the arrival of the Olympus in Singapore was raising some serious issues. Not the least of these was his call to Mr. Lee, the fence in the city.

"Hello, is this Mr. Lee?" David was in a closed phone booth off the hotel lobby.

"Yes, who is this?" came the reply.

"Mr. Lee, how do you like your chocolate syrup?" The code words had been set up by the contact at the Bakkar factory.

"I like my chocolate syrup on vanilla ice cream." Parker could hear the Chinese accent, but the response was correct.

"Mr. Parker, where have you been? I had given up on you. You were supposed to be here over a week ago," Mr. Lee said.

"Yes, I am sorry about the delay. We had an accident on the ship," Parker replied. "I have the diamonds. Can we meet right away?"

"Mr. Parker, I am sorry, but I don't have the cash now. I thought our deal had fallen through. It will take me at least a week to get the money together."

"What? Oh no. I will have to leave Singapore before that."

"Will you be coming back soon?" Lee's question threw him, this was a whole new situation. The plan was coming off the rails.

"Yes, but I don't know when."

"Can you give me at least a weeks' notice? I would really like to do business with you."

"I don't know, let me think about it." Parker's mind was in a whirl. What the hell was he going to do? He hung up the phone and stared vacantly out into the hotel lobby. Two crew members crossed his vision. Suddenly his heart jumped in his chest as he recognized the engineer cadet that had seen him come out of Bakkar's cabin. What was his name? Marlin, that was it. That kid could tell the police what he had seen. Jesus Christ, he was a real threat to the whole plan. As he went back to his room, Parker realized he was in big trouble. Yes, he had the jewels, but if Marlin told the police what he had seen, and the cops were bound to be focused on the Bakkar's cabin, then he would become suspect number one. Back in his room, he was sweating profusely. Could he just flee taking the jewels with him? Disappear into Singapore and wait for a week until he could get the cash. No, that would immediately make him the chief suspect and the police would be looking everywhere for him. And it was tight in Singapore, there weren't too many places to hide that he knew about. And he would need money that he didn't have right now. And then, if he fenced the gems, how would he get out of the city with the cash? They would be watching all modes, road, sea, and air. No, he couldn't see how that would work. Other than giving himself up, and no way was he going to do that, he was left with only one choice. He had to get rid of Marlin. The phone in the room rang.

"Dave, you there?" It was the First Mate's voice.

"Yes, yes, sorry I was in the bathroom. What's up?" Parker tried mightily to keep his voice even.

"You OK, you sound a bit off," the First Mate said.

"I'm fine, had a bit too much to drink last night."

"Yea the local stuff, particularly the beer can get to you. I think they make it with chemicals. Anyway, you'll be out of here Thursday, Nereus is up in Hong Kong and her second mate just went ashore to the hospital with some kind of infection. They need you up there ASAP to take his place. OK?"

"Yes, I suppose so," Parker answered.

"Well, you ought to be happy, Acting Second Mate will be a step up for you and if everything works out well, you could probably get rid of the 'Acting' for your next trip, more money and a better watch. Now you need to catch an early plane Thursday morning. There's a Cathay Pacific flight that leaves Singapore at 0830 arrives Hong Kong at 1525, makes a couple of stops along the way, but it's still the best way to go. Pick your ticket up tomorrow at the hotel concierge's desk, it'll be there waiting for you. It's flight 700Z. Get a cab from the hotel but make sure you get to the airport by 7am." He hung up. The call shocked Parker. If he was going to make it out of Singapore with the diamonds and without the police on to him, he was going to have to come up with something fast to silence Marlin. Every time he thought about what he would have to do, he started to shake. He had never dreamed that the plan to steal the diamonds would ever come to this. He had been in a few punch ups in bars in Liverpool and elsewhere, but he had never really hurt anyone. The use of the empty handgun in Penang was about as far as he had ever gone with a physical threat. Now he was faced with actually killing someone, a young man who was entirely innocent but had been unlucky enough to see something he shouldn't have. He wasn't sure he could do it. He lay on the bed, he could feel a severe headache starting at the back of his head, he had to make a decision, and soon.

Parker went to the hotels guest's office area where there were typewriters, phones, and a fax machine. He typed up a message and addressed an envelope. He put the message into the envelope, sealed it and left it at the front desk. Then he left the hotel and took a cab to the Saint Michaels Bus Terminal and retrieved the diamond bag package from the locker he had rented. He had asked the cab to wait for him and he returned directly to the hotel. Before entering the hotel, he went down the street to a clothing shop and bought a black cotton hat and two large black cotton scarves. He had wanted a ski mask but that wasn't something one could find in Singapore. Then in a hardware type store he bought a large cheap adjustable spanner, heavy enough to cause a fatal blow. Back in his room he wound the scarves around his face, tied them at the back of his neck, and jammed the hat down on his head. He looked at himself in the mirror, he couldn't see any part of his face other than his eyes. It wasn't a perfect disguise, but it would have to do. Even if Marlin did recognize him, he would not live to tell anyone about it. He pocketed the spanner, stuffed the scarves in his pocket and prepared to walk over to the dock.

CHAPTER 23

By Wednesday morning, John Grange and I still hadn't heard where and when we were to be assigned. We both figured we were going to Triton, but maybe she already had cadets on board, and maybe they were struggling with accommodations for us. At breakfast in the hotel's café the second engineer came over to us and said that we would know for certain later that day. We queried him as to where we were going, and he held up his hand as if to indicate that he didn't know. He walked away.

"What in the hell is the big secret?" John said. "He knows where we are going but for some reason, he's not saying."

"I don't think it's certain yet. He's been pretty straight with us so far this trip. Maybe they're struggling a bit." And at about 10.30 am, it became clearer. John and I were going to be split up. I was going to Triton and John was going to wait a few more days in Singapore and then get on Paleamon, a company motor vessel headed back to the UK. A little after the second engineer's call advising us of our assignments, we got a message to go down to the hotel check in desk and pick up messages. I had two and John had one. We both opened a message and found written instructions for our reassignments signed by the Chief Engineer. I was to board Triton at noon on Thursday. John was to stay in the hotel and board Paleamon on Sunday morning. My second message was a bit confusing. It was from the Chief also, although not signed. It directed me to go to the Olympus at 4 pm and report to the lower level of the engine room for a repair task. This seemed strange, I was not aware that anyone, but a skeleton crew, was on the boat, but I figured maybe something special was going to be done and he wanted me there. But why wasn't John Grange instructed to be there also? I didn't understand it, but I wasn't going to start querying the Chief. No, I would go in a boiler suit and see what they wanted me for.

It was about a twenty-minute walk from the hotel to the dock through streets thronged with Chinese, Malays, Indians, and other Asian nationalities. Vendors were plying their food at every corner and unusual, exotic odours were emanating from the pans on their small stoves. Shops were busy selling inexpensive clothing, transistor radios, boom boxes, compact discs, wall mount and desk telephones, and cheap souvenirs. There were numerous barber shops often fronting for what I had been told were massage parlors and brothels, this was after all close to the dock area. At several locations, the road crossed garbage clogged waterways that stank of human sewage. Although Singapore was in many respects much cleaner that other Asian cities, they still had work to do on basic infrastructure. As I boarded the Olympus, she was still where we had berthed, I saw no one manning the gang plank so I went straight to the main deck and entered the top of the engine room. It was relatively quiet in the machine space with only one diesel generator running. I went down the steep steel steps leading to the lower levels and saw no one. There appeared to be no repair work underway. I looked at my watch, it was about three minutes after four. As I walked along the lower level paralleling the main engine, I saw a Pakistani oiler coming around the end of the main engine and walking towards me. His mouth suddenly opened, and his hand came up pointing directly at me. As I turned my head to the right, I slipped on a greasy floorplate. As I went down, I felt a heavy object graze my right shoulder and then I heard a crash as a large adjustable spanner or shifter hit the steel deck. I rolled on to my back to see a masked figure running back to the ladder leading up and out of the engine room. My heart was racing, what had just happened? Someone had tried to nail me. If the oiler hadn't pointed and I hadn't slipped, that spanner would have crashed into the back of my skull.

"You OK, you OK?" The oiler was kneeling beside me on the floorplates. I nodded at him.

"Yes, I think so. I can't believe what just happened."

"That bad man, he tried to kill you. I saw him behind you." His English was not good, and I could barely understand his words.

"Did you see who it was? Did you recognize him?" He looked at me blankly. He had not understood me.

"Do you know the man?" He shook his head in answer to my question.

"Wore mask," and he moved his hand across his face.

The attack was nothing I had ever experienced before. I was shocked to the point of not really believing what had just happened. What had I done to cause someone to come after me with a clear intent to hurt or even kill me? I eventually recovered my wits and went up onto the main deck.

There was a man standing by the gangplank. He was tall with a big beard and I recognized him as one of the deckhands. He certainly was not the man who had attacked me.

"Did you see someone just leave for the dock?" I asked.

"No, I just got back here. I was in the head for a while, case of the heebie-jeebies I'm afraid." He would never admit taking the twenty quid from the deck officer who wanted him gone from the gangplank for fifteen minutes.

"How long were you there?" I asked. He looked at me as if it were none of my business. "Sorry, the reason I'm asking is that someone just attacked me in the engine room."

"There's not supposed to be anyone on board except for a few oilers," he said. "What the fuck are you doing here?"

"I got a message from the Chief Engineer to be in the engine room at four o'clock. I figured some kind of repair work was going on."

"No, no repair work going on right now and there probably won't be until they move her to dry dock. Someone was having you on." That someone I thought, had sent me the message, and then tried to kill me.

CHAPTER 24

When I got back to the ship, I decided I had to call the Chief Engineer. I didn't really want to disturb him, but I felt I had to tell him what had happened. My left shoulder was hurt from falling to the floorplate and I had a long chafing mark which had broken the skin in a few places, on the outside of my right upper arm. They both ached. I was bruised and sore.

"Chief, this is Philip Marlin, sorry to disturb you sir, but I thought you ought to know what just happened to me." I was nervous calling him.

"Go ahead son." He didn't sound annoyed. "I assume it's important or you wouldn't be calling me would you."

"No sir. Anyway, a few hours ago, I got a message with your name at the bottom, it wasn't signed, telling me to report to the engine room of the Olympus at 4 pm. I thought it a bit strange, but I also thought I'd better do as I was told. When I got there, the engine room appeared to be empty. But on the lower level, next to the main engine crankcase, I was attacked by someone who tried to crash a shifter, sorry, a large adjustable spanner, into the back of my head. Fortunately, an oiler, don't know his name, had seen the attacker behind me and pointed to him. Also, very fortunately, I slipped at that moment and the shifter scraped down my right arm before clattering down onto the steel floor plates. I turned to look at the attacker, but he ran away back up the stairs. I questioned the oiler, a Pakistani I think, but he didn't know who it was either. The attacker was wearing a mask over his face, I think he had tied a black scarf round his head."

"Are you hurt son?" the Chief asked with clear concern in his voice.

"Bruised and aching. A little bleeding maybe."

"OK, come on up to my room now. I'm in 409," he said. When I got to his room, he opened the door and I could see several people inside including Captain Mosgrave, another Blue Flags official wearing a Captain's uniform, another man who looked like a medic, and a police officer.

"Marlin, right?" the chief asked.

"Yes sir."

"Captain McDonald, the head of fleet operations is here along with a member of the Singapore police force." I nodded at Captain McDonald. I vaguely knew that he was a very senior person in the company.

"Please take off your shirt, lets look at you," another man said. He had a first aid kit on the table, and he immediately started to swab the chafed cuts on my right upper arm. It stung, but I grinned. "Need to do this to avoid any infection," he said. "I'm going to wrap your arm in a big bandage not because your injury is that bad, but because it's easier to put the one bandage on than a bunch of little ones. I'll give you some smaller plaster type bandages to apply in a couple of days when you take this off. Use this antibacterial cream on each cut. Any other areas I should look at?"

"My left shoulder is bruised and sore but that's all," I said.

"Let me look at it." He moved my arm around as he held my shoulder. "Any pain?"

"No, it's OK, just feels sore," I said.

"Just a bruise, should be good in a day or two."

"OK Marlin, why don't you sit down," the Chief said. "Go over the whole thing again for us and the officer." I repeated the entire story.

"Do you have any idea who did this and why?" the police officer asked. I hadn't had a lot of time to think about it.

"At the moment, I'm a total blank. I guess I'm starting to feel a little shocked. That guy could have killed me," I said.

"You were targeted for some reason," the officer said. "Have you been in a disagreement with someone on the ship or at local bar or something?"

"No, and I haven't been anywhere besides the hotel and the ship. And I can't think of anything that would have annoyed or upset anyone."

"OK, whoever did this to you may try again. So, I want you always to be with someone else when you go out of your room. I understand from Mr. Robinson that there is another engineer cadet that you are rooming with. You and he should go everywhere together until you leave Singapore. You understand?" The officer looked directly at me as he spoke.

"Yes, I understand. This is all a little surreal," I said.

"I'm calling John Grange now, I hope he's in your room," the Chief said. John was and he immediately came up to the Chief's room although it was clear when he entered that he had no idea what was going on. I had not seen him since I had returned to the ship, so he didn't know what had happened to me. "Grange, for reasons that Marlin here will explain to you, I don't want you to let him out of your sight until he leaves Singapore on Triton tomorrow. Got that?" Poor John, he looked gobsmacked, but I smiled at him.

"John I'll explain what is going on when we get back to our room," I said as we left.

"Mr. Robinson and Captain Mosgrave, I believe this has something to do with the stolen diamonds," the officer said. "Marlin doesn't remember it yet, but he's seen something or somebody, that relates to the theft. And the thief or thieves know that and determined that they had to get rid of him. They are obviously extremely ruthless and dangerous. The sooner Marlin gets out of Singapore on one of your vessels the better. I am going to post an officer on the hotel corridor where their room is until Marlin leaves tomorrow. Just a precaution."

"OK, I understand. Can we keep what happened to Marlin quiet? I don't want the rest of the crew talking about this," the Chief said.

"You had better call him and Grange and let them know that this should not be discussed with others." The Chief immediately called Marlin's room and advised him of the need to keep the whole situation to himself and Grange.

"Do you have someone on watch at the gangplank at all times while a ship is docked? I mean, how do you prevent unauthorized people from entering the vessel?" The officer's enquiry was embarrassing to the Chief.

"Yes of course. But that is a deck officer's responsibility, Tony, can you find out who was supposed to be on duty and why both Marlin and his attacker were not seen entering the vessel. As Marlin told us, whoever was supposed to be there had been in the head, the WC, with a case of stomach and bowel upset, for at least fifteen minutes, so it appears the gangplank was unguarded for that time."

"Seems very convenient, doesn't it?" the officer responded. "Captain, please call me as soon as you have any information about this." The officer gave the Captain and the Chief his business card and then left the room.

"My my Tony, if it isn't one thing it's another," Colin McDonald said.

"This is turning into the trip from hell," Mosgrave said. "Have never had a passenger file a complaint like this. Apparently, the gentleman in question was carrying very valuable diamond stones to his agent in the city here."

"Why weren't the jewels in the ship's safe?" Colin asked.

"He claims he has made this trip with jewels on many occasions and preferred to keep them in his direct possession."

"Will he file a claim against us?"

"Probably, but I think the fact he didn't use the ship's safe will be important in our defense."

CHAPTER 25

Bakkar spent a long time on the phone with his partner in Antwerp. Fiona watched him as he nervously described the situation. It was clear that his partner was furious, she could hear his raised voice on the phone from six feet away. Jacob's face was red from annoyance and embarrassment, and at times he had difficulty responding to questions. The call must have a cost a fortune, he was on the line for over an hour.

"That was not pleasant. My partner threatened to wind up the firm and sever our relationship. I have never heard him so annoyed and upset," Jacob said.

"Do you really think he'll do that?" Fiona asked.

"I don't know. Right now, I think he'd like to kill me. I knew he had a temper, but I've never been subjected to its full force before."

"What's he going to do about the theft?" She wanted to know in case it represented any kind of threat to her plans.

"He's going to get the Antwerp police involved. You heard me giving him the number of the Singapore police commissioner, so they'll probably start there. Then he's going to have the Dutch police interview everyone in the office and at the factory. It's going to take some time I suppose. He told me to get the next ship home." Fiona felt good about what was happening, or really what was not happening. There had been no mention of the police wanting to search the passengers formerly on the Olympus. Of course, there were only eleven besides Jacob, but she assumed that they were now, except for herself and the man named Lovett, dispersed all over Asia. She knew Lovett was still in Singapore because she had seen him in the hotel. After Jacob's phone call, they had a late lunch sitting on a terrace adjacent to the hotel's fine dining restaurant, and then Fiona left Jacob sipping a brandy at the table as she went upstairs to their room to start packing. Once in the room, she could hardly contain her inner joy and satisfaction. She had got away with it. No one, least of all Jacob, suspected her. Now she could look forward to a life of ease and comfort. No more worrying about spending money on clothes. When she got to Sydney, she would replenish her wardrobe, and go to the hotel's spa and get herself relaxed and glamorized. It wouldn't be long before she had some rich man in tow. She would like someone who had a yacht or motorboat, who could take her safely out for day trips to exotic beaches and backwaters where they could swim and make love in the open air on the boat's deck. Her mind continued to fantasize on how wonderful her new life would be until her reverie was broken by Jacob entering the room.

"Darling, I was wondering if you might be able to stay a few more days after all. I was talking to the Blue Flags agent on the phone downstairs, and they've got me booked in a single cabin on a ship called the Paleamon leaving for the UK on Sunday. What do you think?" Jacob looked at her expectantly.

"Oh dear, I don't think I can change my plans now. My friend in Hong Kong, Rachel, has arranged a special weekend for us with tours of Victoria and a trip to Macau. Her family is involved, and I would hate to cause them to cancel the whole thing." It was the quickest excuse she could come up with and she knew she would have to do better. "Let me call her and see whether it can be changed. She seemed excited about it when I talked to her yesterday."

"I didn't know you had spoken to her." Jacob looked confused.

"Oh yes, I forgot to tell you that she called the hotel and I spoke to her for ten minutes or so at a phone in the lobby yesterday afternoon. Let me call her in a bit, she is often out doing charity work during the day." Fiona realized that she would either have to fake a call from their room or get out of the room for a while to get away from Jacob and make a fictitious call from the lobby. She preferred the latter scheme but wasn't sure how she could arrange it. She had stopped packing to make it look like she was seriously thinking about changing her plans, but in fact it was the last thing she wanted to do. Then fate stepped in once again, there was a call from the police. They wanted to go over the current status of the investigation and suggested Jacob come to the central police station because the commissioner wanted to attend. Jacob left immediately and her need for a fake call was alleviated. She thought more about what would make it impossible for her to stay. She decided that 'Rachel's' mother and father-in-law were coming from Shanghai specifically to meet her and so she really had to be there starting Friday. She knew Jacob would be upset but she thought he would ultimately understand and relent. She might have to satisfy him again just to make sure.

"The police told me something I don't understand," Jacob said as they ate dinner at the hotel. Fiona looked at him expectantly and with some inner concern. Was she now a suspect? "One of the crew members from the Olympus was attacked on the ship. The police believe that this is, in some way, related to the theft of the diamonds."

"How on earth could that be?" Fiona asked.

"They think the crew member saw or heard something about the theft. And they think the thief or thieves see this crewman as a threat and they tried to silence him this afternoon."

"Oh my god, is the man OK?"

"Yes, he was slightly hurt but on questioning by the police, he can't think of what he might have seen or heard that was linked to the theft." Fiona was amazed at this turn of events. What the hell was going on? The police must suspect another crewmember. Wow, they were way off the true scent. She felt elated, they would never suspect her now.

Jacob was quite petulant about the fact that she wouldn't stay a few extra days. But after she explained the fictitious situation in Hong Kong, he calmed down and they completed their dinner still talking about the theft. When they got back to the room she finished packing and then decided to take a bath. While she was in the tub, she called to Jacob to come and wash her back for her. She knew that this would get him aroused, and as she leaned forward to allow him to lather up her back, she pulled his other hand into her naked cleavage. Then she straightened up and moved her two wet hands to his trouser belt.

"What has got into you tonight?" he said.

"Well, I realized I won't be seeing you for a while." She smiled at him coyly. "Take off your pants." He stopped washing her back and dried his hands on a towel. He dropped his pants.

"Underwear too please," she said. As he pulled down his underpants his erection sprang into sight. She took the flannel and washed his member as water dripped all over the bathroom floor. He was standing next to her and she got on her hands and knees in the tub and took his penis into her mouth. As she lapped and sucked, he started to moan and pulled her head hard against him. She could feel his orgasm building as he thrust more rapidly, and she sucked more vigorously. Then suddenly, he was arching his back and shooting his fluids deep into her mouth as he called her name over and over. She had long ago found the sensation and taste to be acceptable, but the real thrill was knowing that she held power over the man she was ministering to. Men were simple creatures after all, they just wanted their cocks and egos rubbed.

In the morning, she was up early and left the hotel at 6.30 am. As the bellman loaded her luggage into a cab, she looked up at the hotel's façade. She would never see Jacob again and although she didn't understand why, she felt just the slightest tug at her heart. Taking his diamonds was just a business transaction in her mind. She knew he would survive.

"Paya Lebar Airport," she instructed the cab driver.

CHAPTER 26

The Chief Engineer was sitting in a small suite occupied by the Captain of the Olympus. They both were drinking single malt scotch at ten in the evening.

"From what you say Jim, Cadet Marlin was very lucky. He could have been seriously hurt or even killed. I have had some fights on my ships, but nothing quite so cold blooded and evil as this. I still don't understand it."

"The police are convinced it's related to the theft of Bakkar's diamonds," Jim said.

"But you say that Marlin can't think of anything that might be behind the attack?"

"Tony, I think we need to tell Marlin more about the theft. Maybe if he knew it was passenger Bakkar that lost something and that that something was a bag of diamonds, it might trigger something in his memory. We've kept the details close to the chest until now, but I think we should let him know more. What do you think?"

"Yes, but he must be sworn to secrecy. I don't want this whole mess getting into the local press or the papers back in the UK. The owners would not be at all pleased about that." The Chief called Marlin at 7.30 am the next morning.

"Marlin, you're going over to Triton later today, correct?" the Chief said.

"Yes Chief, my instructions were to report there at 12 noon," I said.

"OK, when you've eaten your breakfast, come up to my room at say 9 am, I need to talk to you some more about what happened. You haven't had any more thoughts about who may have done it?"

"No Chief. I'll come up at nine." Why did he want to speak with me again? I had no new information or ideas. It made me nervous. With John Grange, I ate a small breakfast in the hotel's café. "Why does the Chief want to see me again? Am I in some kind of trouble?"

"Well, ya, when somebody tries to whack you on the head, you're in some kind of trouble," John replied. "But the Chief probably just wants you to go over the whole thing again to see whether it jogs your memory or something."

"Could be I suppose. Anyway John, it's been nice knowing you, I'm going over to Triton later this morning, probably won't see each other again until we get to the workshop." The workshop was the third and final part of the sandwich course. After a cadet had done three or four voyages, they would be assigned to the company's workshop in Birkenhead for about twelve months before going to sea as a junior engineering officer. I didn't tell John that I had been thinking seriously about leaving the merchant navy and quitting the course. I had concluded that a seagoing career was not what I wanted to do. So, I would not be seeing him at the workshop.

When I got to the Chief's room, there was once again a police officer with him. My heart dropped, what was up?

"Sit down Marlin. We want to give you a bit more information in the hope that it might stir something in your memory. The officer here will provide the information and take notes on anything you might come up with. But I must caution you, that whatever you are told today must not leave this room. We do not want the details of the theft becoming common knowledge. Understand?"

"Yes Chief." I was very nervous, and my voice didn't sound normal.

"Son, you're the victim here, you don't need to be worried," the Chief said.

"Mr. Marlin, my name is Umar Sayid and I am a detective with the Singapore police department. First let me tell you that we found no fingerprints on the heavy spanner that your attacker used. He must have worn gloves. But we think the attack is somehow related to the theft of a small bag of highly valuable diamonds from a passenger on the Olympus. The passenger's name was Bakkar and he was traveling with a Miss Marchbanks. They boarded the vessel in Rotterdam, and he was carrying the bag on his person when he boarded the ship. Once in his cabin, he stored the bag in a locked suitcase which he kept in a closet. He checked the suitcase regularly every time he left or returned to the room. He claims that he never noticed any possible tampering with the bag."

"Wait," I said. The officer stopped his speech and looked at me. "What cabin number was the person in?" I asked.

"You mean Mr. Bakkar?" the officer asked.

"Yes, Mr. Bakkar." The officer looked down at a notebook before he answered my question.

"He was in cabin four with the lady," the officer said.

"What is it son? Do you remember something?" the Chief's tone was almost sharp.

"I think it was cabin four. It was about the third one on the left of the companionway," I said.

"What was?" the officer said.

"Errr, about three days before we got to Penang, I was on watch in the engine room when the second engineer asked me to deliver a message to you Chief. He didn't want to disturb you, so he asked me to push a note under your door." I started to remember the occasion quite clearly. It was only about ten days ago.

"Yes, I recollect receiving a note from the second engineer," the Chief said.

"Well, as I was walking along the companionway, I saw a deck officer coming out of cabin four, I'm pretty sure it was cabin four. It was dinner time, so I assume the occupants of the cabin were in the dining room. I remember it better now, because he asked me what I was doing on that deck particularly as I was in a boiler suit, and that I should leave immediately. He was short with me even after I had told him why I was there."

"Did you recognize this deck officer?" the policeman asked. "And was he carrying anything?"

"Yes, it was Mr. Parker, the third mate. I knew him because we cadets and the midshipmen normally sat a table with him and the third engineer in the dining room. I don't think he was carrying anything, but I don't clearly remember." The officer looked at the Chief and nodded slightly.

"Let me call Mosgrave and ask him about the cabin location," the Chief said. He picked up the phone and spoke into it almost immediately. After a few minutes of conversation, he put the phone down and disconnected the call.

"Cabin four is the third cabin on the left on the companionway looking towards the stern. Is that the one?" the Chief asked me.

"As sure as I can be about anything that happened at that time Chief, yes that was the cabin."

"Thank you, Mr. Marlin. I have no further questions for you," the officer said.

"Marlin, you've been very helpful. Now remember, no talking about this to anyone. I have asked the second engineer to accompany you over to the Triton leaving here at 11.30. I don't want you unaccompanied anywhere till you are in your quarters on Triton. Have a good rest of your trip," he said as he showed me to the door. As I walked down the hotel corridor to the elevator my mind was whirling. Had Parker stolen the jewels? Was he or some accomplice the person who attacked me because I had seen him coming out of the cabin? It started to finally make sense to me. The bad guys had worked it out that I would eventually wind up telling the police about the chance meeting with Parker outside cabin four. They had tried to get rid of me. Wow, I would be happy to get out of this place and get on the Triton.

CHAPTER 27

"I still don't understand this," the Chief said. "Bakkar claims the bag that should have contained the diamonds was never tampered with. It had never been opened."

"That's probably correct, but it wasn't the bag that originally contained the diamonds. Someone, somehow, substituted an exactly similar bag for the real thing," Umar said.

"But how is that possible?"

"Must be an inside job. Someone at the Bakkar factory must be involved. They somehow got an exactly similar bag, filled it with small pebbles and ultimately got Parker to substitute it for the real bag. Parker may just be a pawn in this heist. Maybe he's just going to get a pay off when he delivers the bag to someone. Who knows?" Umar paused and looked directly at the Chief. "So where is Parker?" he asked.

"I have no idea. He doesn't work for me. Let me call the Captain again and find out just where he is." Robinson called the Captain's room but this time he got no answer. Tony must have stepped out for some reason. He hung up and called the First Mate's room.

"What can I do for you Chief?" came the reply.

"Alex, where is your Third Mate, Mr. Parker? The Chief asked.

"He left this morning for Hong Kong. He's going to fill in for the second on the Nereus. Funny thing though, I tried to contact him last evening just to make sure everything was a go, and apparently he had already checked out of the hotel."

"Alex, I think we may have a serious problem with Mr. Parker. It looks like he may have been involved in the theft on board the Olympus." The Chief wasn't sure how much the First Mate had been told, so he didn't get into particulars.

"You've got to be kidding. I mean we all know David Parker is not a shining star or anything, but I didn't take him for a robber," the First Mate said.

"Worse than that. We think he or an accomplice attacked an engineer cadet in the engine room yesterday. The attacker tried to brain him with a heavy spanner."

"Yes, I had heard about the attack and that out gangplank watchmen was missing." The officer interrupted the Chief.

"We need to know if Parker actually got on the plane. Ask what the airline and flight number is." The Chief repeated the request into the phone.

"Hold on a second, let me look at my assignment list. OK, it's Cathay Pacific flight 700Z scheduled to leave Singapore at 08.30 this morning and arrive Hong Kong at 15.25. What do you want me to do?" The Chief wrote the details on a pad by the phone.

"Nothing at the moment. The police will take care of this. You better get a message to Nereus that Parker is probably going to be unavailable, and they should make alternative plans," the Chief said.

"Shit, oh sorry sir, that probably means I'll have to go up there. Please let me know as soon as possible what is happening with Parker."

As soon as the Chief had put the phone down the policeman came over, picked up the pad and called his office.

"I need Detective Teuku's office, this is Umar." There was a long pause. "Gana, could you please check something for me. Was there a passenger David Parker on Cathay flight 700Z this morning? The flight was supposed to depart Singapore at 08.30 and was headed for Hong Kong. Also check and see whether the flight was due to stop somewhere else before arriving in Hong Kong. Get back to me as soon as possible at this number," he read the hotel's phone and room number from the plate at the center of the phone's dial. He disconnected the call.

"What are you going to do?" the Chief asked.

"We'll detain Parker as soon as he exits the aircraft. Could be in Hong Kong or somewhere else if the plane is making an intermediate stop. We will question him and search his person and luggage. I think he's our man or one of our men. What would he be doing going into Bakkar's cabin? And why did he check out early? I think he might have been the attacker and when that didn't work out, he got out of the hotel fast. Not sure whether he would have got on the flight he was supposed to but certainly that was a quick way to get far from Singapore. But he might have just gone to ground here in the city. We should know soon. You better make the Captain aware of what's going on and he might choose to bring Mr. Bakkar up to speed."

An hour later, Umar Sayid, who had left the hotel and returned to police headquarters, called the Captain.

"Parker is on the flight. We just missed getting him at Bangkok. The plane had taken off for Hong Kong about fifteen minutes before the Thai police were notified. Don't worry, we will get him at Kai Tak."

"You sound even more sure that Parker is the thief," Mosgrave said.

"Yes, he either is the thief or is an accomplice. We think it likely he's carrying the diamonds."

"But why would he follow his assignment instructions and head for Hong Kong, I mean we know where he'll be."

"It's our judgement that the man is a complete amateur. The botched attempt on Marlin's life, the fleeing from the hotel, the use of the ticket he was given to go to Hong Kong. He's floundering around and probably didn't have the means to buy an airline or ship ticket to a different destination. Perhaps he has friends in Hong Kong who he thinks can help him. They could be the people he's supposed to deliver the diamonds to get his payoff. And maybe he's naive enough to think he can just go to the vessel he has been assigned to and report for duty. Anyway, we will pick him up and soon find out if he's innocent or guilty. We are fairly sure it's the latter." The police officer's words were at once calming but also difficult. If Parker had the diamonds, then the Blue Flags Line was likely to be sued by Bakkar for negligence. The Line would counter that the gems should have been kept in the ship's safe, but if Bakkar threatened to go public on the matter, they would probably offer a settlement even if the diamonds were recovered. No, it was not a good situation. He would have to call Bakkar right away and tell him what was going on.

CHAPTER 28

Fiona, now Felicity, arrived at the airport terminal at 7.15 am. Her flight to Sydney was scheduled to leave at 9 am and she didn't want to be rushed. As she exited the cab a baggage porter came over and she directed him to the boot of the vehicle. She had three suitcases, two of which were quite large. But she thought that as a first-class passenger that should not be a problem. She had the diamond bag in her purse, tucked into a zippered side pocket. She looked for the Malaysia-Singapore Airline and then walked to the first-class check-in counter. As she approached the counter, her heart sank. There was a sign saying that the flight was cancelled due an aircraft mechanical problem. At first, she was shocked, what was she going to do? She didn't want to go back to the hotel. Then the shock turned to anger, what kind of an airline was this anyway?

"Can I help you madam." The counter clerk was an attractive Malay man.

"What on earth is happening?" Felicity said. "I have a first-class reservation to Sydney, and I need to get there as soon as possible."

"What is your name madam?"

"Fio—, Felicity Montcrief." She realized she needed to calm down. She didn't need to make any silly mistakes.

"Oh yes madam, we are very sorry for the cancellation of your flight, but we have you booked to Sydney via Hong Kong. I'm afraid you will not get there till early tomorrow morning Sydney time but that is the very quickest we can get you there. I have you booked first-class on a Cathay Pacific flight that departs at 8.30 am and gets to Hong Kong this afternoon. Then I have you first-class on an overnight Qantas flight from Hong Kong to Sydney. I do apologize for the cancellation and I hope this alternative routing will meet your approval."

"Do I have time to make the 8.30 flight, its already 7.45?"

"Yes madam, once you have purchased your ticket, we will direct your luggage to the Cathay Pacific flight. You should have no trouble getting to their gate, it's about ten minutes from here. They know you are coming and will hold the flight for you if necessary." She felt the anger draining from her. This attractive young man had been most helpful, and although it was going to take longer, she would still get to Sydney very soon. She handed him her Montcrief credit card, signed the slip, and checked her three bags.

"Thank you for your help. As I'm sure you could tell, I was most unhappy about the cancellation, but I can see that you have done your best to rectify the situation." She gave him her 1000-watt smile and headed towards the Cathay Pacific gate. The flight was already boarding and being a first-class passenger, she was ushered to the front of the line. As she entered the cabin, she saw that a good-looking man was already seated in 1A, although as she settled into seat 2A, there appeared to be only eight first-class seats and half of them were empty including 2B next to her. The economy class passengers continued to board and pass through the first-class cabin. A man went by her that she thought she had seen before, but she couldn't place when or where. She gave the impression no more thought as she was handed a glass of champagne by the stewardess.

David Parker spent an uncomfortable night on a seat in the airport. He couldn't sleep. His nerves were shot. His attempt to kill Marlin had failed miserably, he knew he really wasn't up to such an action. None of it would have been necessary if they had not been delayed by the engine room explosion. He would have got his money and the Olympus would have left Singapore before Bakkar discovered his gems were gone. Any police investigation would have been much more difficult with the Olympus on the high seas. His plan to disappear in Hong Kong seemed more difficult the closer in time he got to it. He needed some help and he had no one to turn to. He needed to call his cousin, have him contact the man at the Bakkar Company and find out where he could sell some diamonds in Hong Kong without drawing the attention of the police. He wasn't sure what the situation was in Singapore. Had the police identified him as a suspect yet? He trusted that that had not yet happened. In Hong Kong, he had to be able to get off the plane easily, get through customs and then do what? Take a cab to where? These thoughts circled through his brain without any resolution emerging. No, he would have to first call his cousin who could suggest a nondescript quiet hotel where he could lay low for a while. That calmed his nerves a little.

At 6 am he got up and wheeled his luggage to the first café he saw opening. He ordered a full breakfast of cereal, bacon, eggs, sausage, grilled tomatoes, toast, and coffee. He felt a little better after eating and after using the bathroom facilities, he headed to the Cathay Pacific counter where he checked his bags and then went to the gate. There were quite a few people already seated in the gate area and more appeared to be arriving every minute. The flight was going to be over half full. He had a window seat, 22F, and was not looking forward to the overall flight time because with the stop in Bangkok, it was going to take about seven hours. He had a magazine and a book, but he wasn't sure they were going to last for the entire trip. As he waited in line, he suddenly saw the blonde beauty who had been a passenger on the Olympus. She was being ushered to the front of the line now boarding. She must be in first-class, nice if you can get it. She really was a good-looking woman with a great figure. As he went through the first-class cabin, he saw her sitting in the second row next to the window. She looked up at him, but he wasn't sure she recognized him.

As the man in seat 1A returned from the rest room, he smiled at her and leaning on the back of the seat asked if she was headed for Bangkok or Hong Kong.

"Well actually I'm heading to stay with a friend in Hong Kong," Felicity said.

"You'll enjoy it there. It's fascinating part of the world," he responded. She could hear a faint Scots accent in the man's speech.

"Are you headed there also?" she asked.

"Yes, but I'm afraid it's only for work, no play. By the way, I'm Colin McDonald."

"Felicity Montcrief," she replied as she held out her hand.

"Nice to meet you," and he shook her hand gently and then sat back down into his seat.

CHAPTER 29

Jacob Bakkar had been woken by Fiona departing. She had leant down and kissed him briefly as he lay in bed, and then she was gone. He knew he would miss her. He was not looking forward to the return trip to Europe and to dealing with the loss of the diamonds. He drifted back off to sleep and was startled awake by the ringing of the bedside phone.

"Yes, who is this?" He was still groggy. The alarm clock showed 11.15, the stress of the last few days had tired him, but he never normally slept this late.

"This is Captain Mosgrave. Mr. Bakkar but I have some information you should be aware of."

"Oh, yes, have you found the diamond shipment?" Bakkar was now wide awake.

"Not yet, but the Singapore police have a suspect that they intend to detain and search as soon as they can get to him," the Captain said.

"What do you mean, 'as soon as they can get to him'?" Bakkar asked.

"Unfortunately, the suspect was a member of the crew of the Olympus, and he's currently on a Cathay Pacific flight bound for Hong Kong. But he will be detained and searched at the airport when the flight arrives. The police here seem confident that he's the thief or one of the thieves, and that he would likely be carrying the diamonds." Mosgrave waited for a response from Bakkar.

"Are you telling me Captain that this man was a member of your crew?"

"Yes, I'm afraid so."

"But this is outrageous. One doesn't expect to board a ship of a reputable company and expect to be robbed. And I still don't understand what happened. You know the bag was not tampered with in any way. It had not been opened at the top, or cut open, or the seams pulled apart. It was in perfect condition." Bakkar voice was raised.

"But the police believe that the bag was not the one you brought on board in Rotterdam. They believe somehow a counterfeit bag was substituted for the real one," Mosgrave said.

"Wait a minute, the seal on the bag had the Bakkar name impressed. There is nowhere besides our factory where that can be done," Bakkar's tone was incredulous. "You're telling me that someone in our factory was behind this theft."

"Mr. Bakkar, it is the Singapore police that are saying this. I suggest you call the police commissioner and speak to him. I know you have talked to him previously. As soon as I have any additional information, I will relay it to you. Good day," and Mosgrave disconnected the call. He had no wish to continue talking to Bakkar.

At 1.30 pm, Mosgrave received a call from Umar Sayid.

"We have received some disturbing information from Saigon," his voice sounded very sombre.

"From Saigon, why Saigon?" Mosgrave said.

"Flight 700Z disappeared from control center radar about an hour ago. We believe the flight has crashed in South Vietnam."

"Oh my god, are you sure?"

"As soon as I get more information, I will let you know the situation." He disconnected the call.

CHAPTER 30

AVIATION MONTHLY JULY 1972

On Thursday June 15, 1972, Cathay Pacific 700Z, a Convair 880 flight originating at Singapore International Airport, had a stopover at Bangkok's Airport with the final destination being Hong Kong's Kai Tak Airport. At 1242 local time, the flight made contact with Saigon control center. At 1244, the crew made a routine transmission updating the progress of their route, adding that they would expect to reach their next waypoint by 1306. This was the last transmission received from the flight.

The wreckage was located in "lightly wooded" terrain, still burning, not long after Saigon control center lost contact. Although two bodies were retrieved almost immediately, the presence of hostile forces nearby made it very difficult to examine the wreckage in depth. The spread of debris suggested that the airplane had broken into three large sections, with the breakpoints almost exactly along the front and rear of the wingbox, prior to hitting the ground, and the relative closeness of these sections suggested that this breakup had occurred at a low altitude. A helicopter inspection showed the debris, including two engines and the horizontal stabilizer, further away, but could not be reached on foot due to war activity. The aircraft's flight data recorder was recovered and read; it showed that the airplane was flying on course at 29,000 feet at a speed of 310 knots until 1259 local time, at which point the recorded data became nonsensical for 30 seconds before stopping entirely. The airplane was not equipped with a cockpit voice recorder.

Upon examining the available debris, it soon become clear that the airplane had suffered some sort of structural problem and loss of control at cruising altitude, and that the low-altitude breakup was caused by the overstressing of the airplane during an uncontrolled descent. Debris from the center fuselage and right wing root, showed signs of explosive "splash," and the number 3 fuel tank showed signs that it had ruptured prior to the low-altitude breakup inferred from the wreckage distribution. The vertical stabilizer showed signs that it had been struck by "at least one body and possibly some seats," and the horizontal stabilizer also showed signs of being impacted by debris in the air. Many bodies were not recovered, possibly because they had been ejected very early in this sequence. Without being able to better examine the wreckage, and lacking valid flight data from the final moments of the flight, it is not known what exactly happened after 1259. What is known is that some sort of explosive device, likely located within the passenger cabin near the right wingbox, detonated at that time, causing unknown but catastrophic damage to the airplane, including but not limited to the damage found on the horizontal and vertical stabilizer. The airplane likely descended rapidly in an "erratic" manner. At an undetermined point in this descent, the horizontal stabilizer separated from the airplane entirely, and eventually the fuselage broke into the three sections initially found by searchers.

A total of 71 passengers and 10 crew members were killed. There were no survivors.

EPILOGUE

Following a UK Civil Aviation Authority and Hong Kong police investigation of the airliner crash, as well as six years of reporting by a Bangkok Post journalist, a police officer whose fiancée and daughter were aboard flight 700Z was charged with placing a bomb on the airliner. Somchai Chaiyasut, who had taken out three travel insurance policies on his fiancée and daughter, was declared not guilty due to lack of evidence. He sued the insurance companies and received 5.5 million baht (approximately US$ 275,000) but died of cancer in 1985 after airline staff and relatives had considered hiring a hitman to kill him.

Philip Marlin quit the merchant navy and the Blue Flags Line at the end of the voyage on the Olympus and Triton. After a year working at a folding box company, he went to university and after gaining a bachelor's degree in mechanical engineering, he took a job at a large corporation in Pittsburgh, Pennsylvania. Tom Parker was devastated by his cousin's death and even more so because the diamonds had been lost in the crash. He resigned from Blue Flags and became the night manager at a hotel in Blackpool, Lancashire. Jacob Bakkar and his company survived the loss of the diamond shipment but had to lay off half their employees including Karel and many experienced diamond cutters. He never heard from Fiona Marchbanks again, and in his mind there developed a deep suspicion that somehow, she had taken the gems. Bakkar married a Dutch girl and subsequently had three children. He never traveled on a Blue Flags ship again. The investigations by the Singapore and Antwerp police eventually identified David Parker as the likely thief. His death caused the case to be dropped. The diamonds were never recovered. Felicity Montcrief's account at the Commonwealth Bank of Australia, was seized by the central government after it had remained dormant for seven years. The value of the account at time of seizure in 1979, was 475,642 Australian dollars. Mary McDonald returned to the city of her berth, Edinburgh, and three years after her husband's death, she remarried. In 1985, due to changing conditions in the shipping industry including the switch to containerization and large vessels, Blue Flags declared bankruptcy and ceased to exist. All its ships were either sold to foreign carriers or broken up.

www.ingramcontent.com/pod-product-compliance
Lightning Source LLC
LaVergne TN
LVHW041706060526
838201LV00043B/607